D1231880

life in the rainbow

life in the rainbow

richard horan

Steerforth Press

SOUTH ROYALTON, VERMONT

For information about permission to reproduce selections
from this book, write to: Steerforth Press L.C., P.O. Box 70,
South Royalton, Vermont 05068.

Library of Congress Cataloging-in-Publication Data
Horan, Richard, 1957–.
Life in the rainbow / Richard Horan. — 1st ed.
p.   cm.
ISBN 1-883642-02-7
1. Group homes for the mentally ill—Illinois—Chicago—Fiction.
2. Nurses' aides—Illinois—Chicago—Fiction. 3. Chicago (Ill.)—
Fiction.   I. Title.
PS3558.0662L54   1996
813'.54—dc20   95-47954 CIP

Manufactured in the United States of America
First Printing

for all of them

Da 34th te Mth eary ʎɹɐпɹpɐꓕ 349

Mother, save your poor son! Shed
a tear on his aching head! See how
they're torturing him! Press a
wretched orphan to your breast!
There's no place for him in this
world! They're persecuting him!
Mother, have pity on your poor little child . . .
And did you know that the Dhey of
Algiers has a wart right under his nose?

Nikolai Gogol
Diary of a Madman

beppe an'a de queena sophia
(a manifesto)

"Long time 'go dere was'a jus'a one an' hill in dee whole worl'. An'a dose anz work'a alla dee time, in an'a out dee an' hole, carryin'a dee food, watchin'a dee eggs, fixin' up'a dee home. Den one'a day a young an', 'bout you age, suddenly stop'a work, put'a down what it is he'a carryin', an'a t'ink'a to himself, 'Why my work'a so hard alla de time? Ev'ry day it'a dee same t'ing—work'a, work'a, work'a.' Meanatime, his'a brudder anz go by him in a line carryin' all sorts t'ings—little piece dead mouse, part'a dee nose, estomach, eyeballs—"

"What?" I squawked at this image.

"Food. Anz eat'a ev'ryt'ing, 'specially dead an'mals; dead two, tree days. Anyways, Beppe, dat'a dee anz name, he begin to stop'a his brudders an'a ask dem why dey work'a so hard, 'Hey, Ludovico,' he call, 'why you carryin'a dat piece estomach? Why you work'a so hard?' he ask him. An'a Ludovico say he'a work hard to support dee Queen. An' Beppe ask him why he care'a so much 'bout dee Queen. He say, Ludovico say, because dee Queen his mother, she ev'rybody's mother, dee Queen. Beppe continue to ask alla dee other brudders which walk'a by why they work'a so hard alla dee time, an' dey all say dee same t'ing—for dee Queen."

"What's the queen's name again?" I just had to slow him down to savor the words for a moment.

"Queena Sophia."

"Queen Sophia," I repeated in my absurd, accentless tongue.

"Yeah, Queena Sophia. *Allora,* den Beppe start scratchin'a his head. Yeah, he know 'bout Queena Sophia an'a ev'ryt'ing like'a dat, but he still no un'erstan' why he an'a ev'rybody half'a work like dey work so hard for her. He can' figure it out."

He stopped cutting my hair, and looked at me as if to say, "Now'a you ask question."

"So what did he do then?" I easily took the hint.

"Dee only t'ing he must'a do. Talk'a to dee Queen. Sure. He tell'a his uncle who guard dee Queena Sophia door, he need'a talk to dee Queen an'a ask her question. His uncle Vanni, that his uncle's name, he big surprise.

"'Why you need talk'a dee Queen?' he yell.

"'Because I must do,' answer Beppe.

"'What you must do? You must do work, not'a ask question. Beside, Queena Sophia no talk'a to you kind'a people.'

"Beppe was stubborn boy. 'What'a you mean my kind'a people?' he angry ask.

"'I mean you kind'a people which'a work. You worker, you no need'a ask question from dee Queen.'

"'But I t'ought dee Queen my mudder? I t'ought I do alla dee work for dee Queen, make her happy because she my mudder?'

"'Da's right, she you mudder, an'a she need you work'a, not ask'a question.'

"'But I wanna ask question. She my mudder an'a I wanna ask her.'

"'She busy. You uncle Venanz in dere now, he'a talk to her an'a other t'ings you know nuttin' 'bout.'

"But Beppe no take no for an answer, an'a when his uncle Vanni back turn, he push his way into dee Queen's'a room. Dere he saw'a dee Queena Sophia, tree times'a big as Beppe, sittin' onatop pile eggs. She'a beautiful, like mountain of red prosciuttos an'a ripe melons, an'a other t'ings like'a dat. His uncle Venanz jus' 'bout to climb up'a dee pile eggs when Beppe come in. Dee Queena Sophia look at Beppe shock; Venanz he's a look shock; dey bot' starin' at'a Beppe shock.

"'What you doin' here?' his uncle Venanz angry ask, talk'a wit his hanz, big wavin.'" Nick imitated the action.

"'I wanna talk wit dee Queen, my mudder.' Beppe say.

"'You can' do dat. You jus' worker, you no can' ask'a question of dee Queen.'

"'Venanzio, *stai zitta*. Quiet!' she's a say. 'What is it my son?' Dee Queena Sophia look'a down sweetly at'a little Beppe.

"'I have question ask'a you, Queena Sophia, my mudder.'

"'Ask'a me, I'm'a you mudder, you ask anyt'ing'a you wish.'

"'Whya we work alla dee time? Whya you need us work alla dee time so hard?' Beppe ask her.

"Dere was big silence. Dee Queena Sophia open her mout', but nuttin'a come out. Uncle Venanz he's a look twice angry as before. He's a growl—'What kind'a question you ask? I slap'a you face. You tryin' be wise guy wit' dee Queen?!'

"'No, I jus' no un'erstand why we work alla dee time,' Beppe say innocent.

"'You lazy, dat's all. You lazy good for nuttin'. You should'a be 'shamed.'

"'Venanzio please,' dee Queena Sophia say. 'He's'a right. Dee *bambino's* right, we alla work'a too much. Look'a how my antennas all wrinkle now. Too much'a dee work.' An'a she make dee sexy eyes at'a Venanz.

"Again it was'a big quiet. Venanz lookin' back'a an'a fort'

at'a Beppe an'a dee Queena Sophia, an'a Beppe lookin' back'a an'a fort' at'a dee Queena Sophia an'a Venanz, an'a dee Queena Sophia jus'a worry 'bout how she look."

I was laughing here.

"Finally Beppe break'a dee silence. 'But why we need'a work so much?' he ask.

"'I don'a know,' dee Queena Sophia say. 'I don'a know why. We always jus'a work hard since I remember. Da's how it suppoza be.'

"Beppe don'a know what to say. Uncle Venanz jus'a stan' lookin' angry at'a Beppe, his long antennas'a tappin' dee floor nervous like'a rain storm. Dee Queena Sophia she's a sit up dere as'a big'a house, listenin' to her own'a words echo 'round. You could'a hear'a pin fall.

"'Well maybe we need'a work less. Maybe we need'a do less work,' Beppe say.

"'You right,' dee Queena 'gree. 'Less work. How much less'a work?' she suddenly ask him.

"'Half'a much,' Beppe say.

"'Half'a much? *Va bene,* half'a much. You tell you brudders dey work'a half a' much from now on.'

"'T'ank'a you Queena Sophia my mudder, t'ank'a you,' Beppe say wit' a bow, an'a he leave, jus'a like dat."

Nick at this point stopped and rolled his shoulders again, looking for encouragement from me in the mirror. Of course my face was the spitting image of a raptured child's. I remember him taking a handkerchief out of his pocket and running it over his smooth and shiny scalp as if he were cleaning the playing surface, like an umpire sweeping off the plate.

"Well, then what happened?" I was playing the dutiful listener's role.

"Jus'a like dee Queen say, dey work half'a much. Dey get up late in dee mornin', lots'a coffee breaks durin' dee day, nice'a relax meal at'a night. Half'a much work, jus'a like dee Queen say." He paused.

I recited my line: "So was that better?"

"Sure it better. Half'a much work mean twice'a much time relax. Dey alla take their time, not work'a so hard. Beppe become big c'lebrity. Ev'rywhere he go, people wave at him, say, 'Hey, Beppe! *Cosa fai?* What you doin'? He dee boss; walk'a roun' like dee rooster. But ev'ry silver cloud have its'a dark inside, like'a dey say, an'a one day somet'ing go wrong. Biga wrong. *Formichiere!* You know what is *formichiere?*"

"No idea."

"An'asucker. An'asucker come 'long wit'a his big nasola an'a suck dee anz up. Put his big nasola inato dee hole an'a ZZZZIP, up'a dey go like'a water t'rough straw. But dis trag'dy should'a be no big'a deal, it's a nat'ral, happen many time's 'fore. Dee an'asucker eat until he full an'a he go his way home. But wit' half'a much work, dat mean half'a much anz in dee hole."

"Wait a minute. I'm not quite following," I queried.

"What I mean say is wit' dee anz workin' half'a much, dee Queena Sophia she make a half'a much eggs. An' before when dee an'asucker eat until he full, dat mean he eat only half'a dee anz in dee hole, dere so many anz. Now, he a suck'a up dee entire hill for a good meal. No anz lef' but a Beppe an'a dee Queena Sophia. Beppe was out sleepin' un'er a tree, dee Queena Sophia so big she no could'a fit outta dee hole." He stopped and shook his head, chuckling a perfectly theatrical, disappointed chuckle.

"Well, how did it end up? What happened to Beppe and Queen Sophia?" I was anxious for the end.

"Beppe an'a dee Queena Sophia work twice as'a hard as before when dey work twice as'a hard. So I guess you could say dey work four times'a hard. Dey make'a eggs an'a eggs an'a more eggs, which make'a more an'a more an'a more anz. Dey never stop'a for break. An'a to dis day dey work'a like dat. An' 'at'sa why we alla work so hard."

"Why's that, because there's a big anteater out there just

waiting to suck us all up?" I kidded him.

"Don' be funny. No, 'cause'a nature say we mus' work' hard like dat."

He was finished with both my hair and the story, and he drew the apron off me slowly, thoughtfully, letting the hair droppings fall ever so delicately to the floor. Folding the apron in three quick movements, he walked slowly and thoughtfully over to his counter and unhooked the tubular vacuum, the machine starting up with a buzzing whir.

"Nature, hunh?" I said loudly over the vacuum.

"Yeah, nature. 'At'sa why we mus'a work," he nodded and probed inside my shirt with the suction tool, concentrating on his work.

"Formicelli, hunh?"

"*Formichiere,*" he corrected.

I started laughing. Suddenly the vacuum nozzle was in front of my face, menacing. "Big nozzle, hunh?"

"Big nasola," he corrected as the nasola came next to my ear with a deafening hum.

preamble

The preceding tale marked the beginning of my adult life, and like Beppe after the *formichiere,* I've been working nonstop and in quadruple time ever since. Nick the Barber told me the story while cutting my hair. The impetus for the telling of the tale was a callow comment I had made about work and Uncle Henry David Thoreau. I had just sauntered into town and had happened into his shop from the street. Once in the chair, I let slip I was looking for a job. Right away he began describing his son-in-law who worked for the city in some god-forsaken capacity. I forget what it was, but boy, did it sound boring. After a point I just couldn't help from blurting out—

"Work, work, work, that's all we do! That's all anyone ever thinks about! Don't you ever get tired of work? Just look out that window, everybody's racing around. You ever hear of the writer Henry David Thoreau? He said he could work just six weeks and live off the money he had made from those six weeks for the rest of the year."

"He stupid man. Six'a week! Ha ha ha, what'a he do, work'a in a gold mine, find'a hun'red pounds gold?"

"No, he was a farmer and a writer."

"He count'a dee writing as'a work?"

"No."

"Then'a he liar. Look'a dat: he write a book, you read'a dee book, he make'a money from that, but he no count'a that as'a work."

"Yeah, I mean no, I don't think he got paid for the books right away," I said, feeling for some reason an obligation to defend my Uncle Henry David against Nick the Barber, a stranger.

"Ev'ry man gotta work hard." He put the conversation back on track. "At'sa what life 'bout, no'a 'ceptions."

"You think so? All this work. The Puritan work ethic. But we're all just working machines, we don't even think about why or what for, we just work to make money, and that's not what life's about if you ask me. Don't you ever get tired of work? Don't you ever feel like all you do, all anyone does is work?"

"You serious, buddy? Work'a dee key. Work'a ev'ryt'ing in'a life. Man have nothing wit'out'a work."

"You believe that? You don't think we work too much."

"Abs'lutely not. Like'a dee anz story, Beppe an'a dee Queena Sophia. 'At'sa what life's 'bout, you cananot change dat. Work's'a nat'ral. Work's'a respons'bility."

"Beppe and the Queen Sophia? Is that a fairy tale?"

"Dee story 'bout anz. You never no hear dee story?"

"No."

"Famous story."

"What's it about?"

"You wanna hear dee story?"

"Yeah."

"Ha ha ha, you no never hear dee story 'bout Beppe an'a dee Queena Sophia?"

"Never."

He smiled broadly. He'd probably been waiting for a sucker like me for months so he could launch into that goddamned tale.

Anyway, after the story we got to talking about me again. My hair all cut, I had him shaving my face.

"So what you do, my buddy?" he asked me.

"Nothing. I've worked in a hospital as an orderly. I've painted houses, worked as a laborer, same as any other lout."

"You? You no look'a like labor to me. You look'a like college boy, young lawyer somet'ing."

"Nope. Not me. I've got a college diploma though. It's in the bottom of my backpack."

"In dee bagpack! You foolin', right?"

"No, I'm serious."

He stopped shaving me for a moment and studied me in the mirror.

"You got college diploma?"

"Yeah."

"An'a you no know what'a you want do? 'At'sa no good." He began shaving again, shaking his head from side to side, a look of reproach on his classically European mug. "No no, 'at'sa no good."

"Well, actually I did know what I wanted to do. I was going to walk from Boston to Alaska and get a job on a fishing boat and then write a book, but I only made it this far."

"What? What you tellin' me? You walk'a here from Boston? Boston, Massachusetts? You'a jokin' me?"

"I'm serious. I walked. Yes sir. Remember Uncle Henry David Thoreau, the guy who worked six weeks a year?"

"Oh yeah, sure."

"Well, I took his words literally. He wrote a book called *Walking* and it went something like this: 'If you are ready to leave father and mother, and brother and sister, and wife and child and friends, and never see them again . . . if you have paid your debts, and made your will, and settled all your affairs, and are a free man, then you are ready for a walk.'"

He stood transfixed, looking at me in the mirror with the widest eyes, incredulous at my recitation. "That was my manifesto," I explained. "I did that, just like Uncle Henry explained. Took care of business and walked, bound for Alaska. But I only made it as far as here—Chicago."

"So you walk'a here from Boston you say? Nick never knew nobody walk'a like that." There was silence. "Why you wanna go 'Laska? Big'a cold place. Nobody live there but'a dee bears an'a eskimo. Better you stay here in'a city where there lots peoples, even'a though it cold place too, not like'a *bella Napule.*" He was shaving delicately the very sensitive area under my nasola. I had to hold my breath. "So you wanna job. Jus'a job. You must'a have talent, dreams'a, somet'ing? You got college diploma."

"Sure, I've got lots of dreams like everybody else, Nick," I said wistfully.

"Dreams'a good. Dreams'a come true you keep'a try hard. This shop a dream. Patience dee key. Must be patient. What'a dreams you got?"

"I'll tell you. I'd like to see the world, and then one day write a book. A good book. A Russian book. None of this clever, boring, effete stuff."

"Ha ha, that's right, you say that before, you wanna write book. 'At'sa good one. Ev'rybody have'a good book he can'a write, even Nick. Peoples, 'at'sa what books 'bout. Even Nick, hear lots'a stories 'bout peoples, 'bout their lives standin'a right here cuttin' hair, shavin'. They tell'a me ev'ryt'ing like I was a priest in'a confession: 'Nick, I cheat on'a my wife, young girl half'a my age, I canna say no.' 'Nick, I bet t'ree t'ousand on'a horse; lose it all.' 'Nick, my daughter she screwin' 'round wid a black boy.' I hear ev'ryt'ing standin'a right here like dis now.

"You wanna write book, you no need travel dee worl', go to cold empty place like'a 'Laska, I tell'a you dat. You jus' need'a be wit' peoples. Lots peoples, int'resding peoples."

He stopped shaving me and looked at me in the mirror pointing the spoon-like razor at my image, his lips pursed. "You wanna meet int'resding peoples? You work in'a hospital?

Then you come'a wid me to dee asane asylum where I work Wednesday when dee shop'a close. *Manicomio.* Asane asylum. *Madonna,* dee poor peoples dere. But each one half'a story to tell. That dee place meet peoples, int'resting peoples."

"You work in an asylum."

"No no, I no work dere 'xactly, I jus'a go once mont' cut'a dee hair is all. Eight dollar a head. Int'resding peoples, *Madonna.*"

"That must be rough, hunh?"

"Rough? What'a you mean rough? You face rough. Those'a poor peoples half'a sad life, live on dee other side life's all. Ev'ryt'ing upside down for them. But that don' mean they no wort' nothin', that don' mean they no human bein's. They live in'a diffren' world. Ev'ryt'ing upside down," he responded rather defensively.

"Wow."

"Yeah, wow. You wanna be writer, see dee worl', un'erstand'a peoples, you start'a wit' them. 'At'sa dee place start. T'ousands stories dere. 'At's'a dee place where you find dee stories, no'a 'Laska."

I took him up on the offer and accompanied him one week later to the "asane asylum" and inquired about a job. A week after that I was dressed in white and reporting for my first day of work as a nurse's aide. He was absolutely right, interesting people, and "ev'ryt'ing upside down."

players, rules, and objectives

As it happened, I arrived at the Rainbow more or less hand in hand with the profit motive. The home had just abandoned its status as a Title XIX facility. A Title XIX is a state-run, Medicaid-funded nuthouse (virtually extinct today). Around about the time I came on board, a private investor had just bought the place. What a gal! A woman about fifty-five, she was a behemoth—six-feet-three and 250 or so pounds of unloved, unromanced, obdurate zeal. There is a rather common expression to describe someone of her ilk—she had a chip on her shoulder. Why? Her height, men; of course the two went together. In fact, it went beyond a chip on the shoulder—that's what it was at first, during her childhood—but it had evolved into a snow-capped misanthropy. Since she'd always been inhuman in stature most of her life, it was natural for her to treat inhumanely all the little creatures that flitted under her nose. She would unexpectedly amble into the building at odd hours to intimidate and bully all the fauna in her ken, her heavily perfumed body stinking up the joint. Mount Shirley, the resident nomenclator, once burst out, "She looks like that Sesame Street character, Big Bird." And so she was dubbed from that day forward. We all walk through life with the sound of a certain kind of song in our heads. For Kelvin, the other aide, it was a rap song; for Nick, an old Italian folk song heavy on the accordion; for someone like my father—Jack Jones's "Call Me Irresponsible"; for Big Bird, unquestionably Strauss's *Also Spracht Zarathustra*. She was the bad guy all right, spelled with a capital B.

And the first thing she did with her new acquisition was to give the place a makeover. Starting with the outside of the building, she had the old bricks sandblasted and painted white. Next, to announce to all her twisted insomniacal obsessions, she had a three-dimensional rainbow painted across the entire building. It started from the lower southern corner, bisected the entire side, curved around to the front, hitting its apex above the entrance, then swung around and back down the northern side to the ground again. Then, she had the down-stairs wallpapered, and flowers, potted plants, and, yes, even tropical fish added.

But this was just an exercise in impatience, because the only possible way for her to get her hands on any filthy lucre was to get rid of all those penniless psychotics and stock the place with private paying clients. She was hip to that from the start. But it was a problem. You couldn't just expel people, they had their rights—money or no money, marbles or no marbles. However, if you could document evidence and prove that certain individuals were a danger to themselves or others, you could then have them shipped out to the county facility with its 2,500 beds and locked wards.

Thus began the war of the Rainbow—the owner and her hired guns versus the aides and clients. As for her hired guns—Paul was enemy number one. He was the floor nurse, and the floor nurse in any institution of valitudinarianism is the absolute sovereign. Paul was the type of person you naturally disliked because he so obviously disliked himself. A very unhappy, roly-poly, still-living-with-mommy forty-year-old with bad teeth and a puffy face that could turn the reddest shade of red imagin-able. He was gay, too, not that that is contemptible, but he was an unhappy gay who had never completely come to terms with his own sexuality—a sign of stupidity in my book. He was a tough customer though, moody and unpredictable, and aware of everything everywhere at all times. He knew it too. In fact, that was his one and only weakness: he thought he knew more than he did. He was allied with the powers that be simply because of his belief that he was smarter than the rest of the world, and he'd be damned if he was going to lose his job on account of some looney or ignorant nurse's aide.

Then there was Gloria, the rat. She had a way of standing and watching a roomful of her subjects with her arms held up at chest level and her hands dangling there, resting back on her heels just the way a rat looks in profile when it stops to sniff the air. She was rabid with her greasy straight black hair, hawkish beak and nasalized voice, all five foot one of her. She was the head nurse, with only one purpose in life, to please the boss. That was it, she had no thoughts other than that, a totally one-dimensional person. She wasn't married, she was asexual as far as I could tell, and she too lived at home with mommy and was about forty. Actually, now that I think of it, Paul and she were a perfect pair—Laurel and Hardy, only with a sinister bent.

Finally there was the poor, pitiful Dr. Comfort, the doddering psychiatrist whom life had completely reamed out so that she shuffled about with her bad hip and bad back and bad eyes in a type of heard-it-all-seen-it-all-before boredom. Who knows what motivated her to comply with the desires and aspirations of the owner, to fulfill her duty as exterminator. Maybe it was the idea that by committing such gross violations of her profession something might come unstuck, the boredom and torpor might suddenly pop off her. Or maybe she just needed the money, her retirement checks simply not being adequate. Or maybe it was because she too was tall, over six feet—there being some arcane six-footers-plus female sorority that stuck together no matter what. Who knows . . . but they had their hands full, I'll tell you, because the aides and the clients were in allegiance against them. We all knew what was up. Every client, psychotic or not, knew the scoop instinctively. And with the aides dressed in full panoply, we were ready to battle to the death.

I submerged myself completely into the work. First, I got my own apartment on the east side of town, right around the corner from the place. A loft. No phone. No parents, no friends. I was incommunicado with the rest of the world, and that's the way I wanted it. Nick was right, why did I want to go to some place so cold and empty as Alaska when I could seclude myself in a forest right in the middle of the city? Besides, at Walden Pond, Thoreau was just a hop skip and a jump from the house of his mentor, Uncle Ralph Waldo.

At first it was like any job I'd had before i.e., forty hours a week, more work than I could aptly handle, too many supervisors. I enjoyed it, though, most of it. In fact I found working in a nuthouse to be a lot like a sporting event. There were officials dressed in white who controlled the action, and, of course, there were the players. Points were scored by:

1. A well-made bowel movement in the appropriate place.
2. Compliance.
3. Non-combativeness.
4. Proper grooming techniques.
5. Eating well.

Fouling was simply a list of opposites:

1. A well-made bowel movement in the inappropriate place.
2. Non-compliance.
3. Combativeness.
4. Improper grooming techniques.
5. Not eating or eating and throwing up.

I considered myself an official at one of those games. I was there for nine months. Nine months, 7:00 A.M. to 3:30 P.M., Monday through Friday. I was a nurse's aide, all dressed in white.

dorothy and amelia

"Hello young man, you're new around here."

"Yes I am."

"Well it's nice to meet you, I'm Amelia Spear. I live in that room over there," she pointed back over her shoulder at the room to her left, my right. Dorothy stood next to her, watching me closely, studying my facial expressions. "Oh my, look at how I'm dressed. I'm so embarrassed. Excuse me."

"Sure."

Dorothy didn't bother to watch her walk away and disappear into her room. Instead, she continued to study me, biting her lip to supress a smile. When Amelia was out of sight, I gave Dorothy a look like—"What's she doing here?"

"She seem fine to you, right?" Dorothy interpreted, her teeth beginning to show.

"Yeah."

She began to laugh in that deep South, drawling laugh of hers. "She the worse on the flo', Richud. The worse. Oh she awful. One minute she nice as pie, actin' like she be goin' to work in the monin', then the nex' minute she crazy out of her mine. She got the Ole Timer's disease."

This was my first day on the job and everything was new to me except Dorothy, a forty-five-year-old motherly black (purple black) lady who must have been my wife or mother in a past life because she seemed so familiar. Amelia was one of the nine women Dorothy was responsible for. There were twenty-nine clients in all up on the third floor where we worked, so Kelvin and I had twenty men to share. Amelia was the only client on the floor with her own room. This was not due to numbers or money, it was due to the "Ole Timers disease" as Dorothy referred to it. Amelia was about sixty, with dirty blonde hair, blue eyes, and delicate features. She looked like a school teacher, and upon first sight, as illustrated, she seemed perfectly normal.

As time went by, this woman who initially impressed me as being of sound mind, far out performed Dorothy's description of her. Some mornings she'd eat breakfast with the rest of the clients, quietly, daintily, cordially, then other mornings she'd be in her room naked, screaming bloody murder and ready to bite, scratch, or kick anyone who approached her. And poor Dorothy had to deal with her every day. Kelvin and I had our banes, e.g., Fred and Megs and Bobby and Leslie Wilder, but I'd take all four of them any day over Amelia.

Amelia's husband used to come and visit her everyday, but he had recently stopped coming when, as Dorothy informed me, "She start to call him by another man's name. She had a lover, tha's why. The Ole Timer's like drink, Richud, the true colors comes out in a person."

Ole Timer's indeed. . . . In her past Amelia Spear had been a vital person. A mother of three, she ran a little antique doll shop downtown, made many of the costumes and clothes herself; even sold dried flowers and cards on the side, all of which she crafted by hand. "I remember her, Richud. She had a nice bi'ness there, always full o' people. Had the nicest window display you ever did see befo' Chris'mas. She a talented lady," Dorothy recalled tisk-tiskfully.

The Dorothy vs. Amelia battles were like squalls or hurricanes. Their ferocity would blow through the place at a hundred miles an hour, then a sudden calm would descend and Amelia would act like a lady, but in a few minutes the wind would pick up and the storm would resume. Dorothy, sweet Dorothy, was a bulldog. She never gave up. Even on Amelia's worst days, Dorothy would uphold the duties of her vocation and tenaciously feed and clothe and bathe that monster.

One day both Kelvin and I were trying to help Dorothy, who was having a hell of a time with her. Amelia was naked, standing on her bed menacing us all with a wire coat hanger. She was hissing and spitting and calling us every name imaginable. We were trying to grab her and coax her and intimidate her. Nothing worked. Then Kelvin called a halt to the charade.

"Time out." He motioned to Dorothy and me to follow him out into the hall. "She ain' gettin' down offa that bed 'less we leave her 'lone for a minute." All three of us were breathing a little faster than normal. Dorothy and I stood looking at Kelvin, the tallest of the three of us. "I got an idea. Rich, close her door." I closed the door. This was what Kelvin did best, come up with ideas. "Now she was one of them suburban white women, no offense Rich."

"No."

"They always gettin' knocks on the door from the UPS mayn or the mailmayn fo' packages 'n' shit."

"Whachu gettin' at, chile?" Dorothy frowned, looking at Kelvin like he was crazy himself.

"I show you. Watch dis." He straightened himself like he was readying to meet the mayor. He rapped loudly on the door. Heads in the day room behind us all jerked around at the sound. It was an impressive knock, an official-sounding knock. There was silence behind the door. He knocked again. We heard scurrying inside the room.

"Who is it?" Amelia asked in the whitest white woman voice I'd ever heard. Dorothy's frown instantly transformed into one of great admiration.

"The UPS man. We have a package for you," Kelvin answered whitemanishly.

"Oh dear, just a minute please." We all three of us leaned our ears to the door listening to the hurried activity going on within.

"You good," Dorothy whispered, smiling brightly at Kelvin. We continued to listen. "Now whachu gonna do when she come to the do'?"

He frowned. He looked around. "Where her breakfas'?"

"I'll get it," I said because I had just seen it lying on top of the nurse's station counter. I retrieved it and handed it to him.

He knocked again. "Come on lady, I don' have all day." Dorothy was right, he was good.

"Coming," she sang.

The door opened with a flourish. There stood Amelia in a patterned dress, earrings on, lipstick, high heeled shoes. She was June Cleaver all over again. She was smiling, looking expectantly at the three of us, Kelvin in the middle holding the tray.

"Well, where is it?" she asked.

"Here it is, yo' breakfas', jus' like you ordered. Nice juice, toas', two eggs."

She looked down at the breakfast tray, and scowled. Then she looked up at Kelvin. "I didn't order breakfast."

"Sho' you did. Here it is."

She shook her head and at that, tipped the tray over and slammed the door. Dorothy began to laugh uncontrollably.

"Cold blooded," Kelvin whistled, his shirt all wet from the juice, the toast and fried eggs scattered about his sneakers. He turned to me—"If I had a package, it woulda worked."

when john brown's face fell

John Brown was the prize specimen, the number-one creature in the kingdom. He hadn't a hair on his body and his steel-gray eyes could look in two different directions at the same time. He was a skeleton come to life with a weird coating of a white, paper-like substance containing his organs, fluids and bones. He was the one who, if they had decided to conduct tours, would have been the main attraction.

" . . . And now ladies and gentleman, John Brown."

"Agh!"

"Oh my God!"

"EEEK!"

"Take a close look now, don't be frightened. Notice the eyes, how they can look at two of you at the same time. See that? And his skin, feel his skin, don't be afraid. Touch it."

"Agh!"

"Oh my God!"

"EEEK!"

"Feels just like paper, doesn't it? Now, can anyone diagnose his disease? Certainly there is one of you who can venture a guess? No one? Then I'll just have to tell you. He is afflicted by one of the world's rarest diseases—Progeria. Can anyone tell me what Progeria is? No one? It's otherwise known as the

'Aging Disease.' People with Progeria have been known to die of old age at the ripe and tender age of three. John Brown, how old are you?"

"I'm worried about my mother. I'm worried about my mother. I'm worried about my mother."

John Brown had been institutionalized most of his life, a product of a system which believed that the best way to treat a wayward mind was to zap it into compliance with electricity.

No, John Brown was not a very good player. He was most often non-compliant, frequently combative if you invaded his space, a picky eater, and an improper dresser. His only redeeming quality was his bowel movements, not one of which I ever witnessed. . . . Perhaps he never had them. I didn't know, and I didn't care to know. He had his space which he guarded faithfully and tirelessly, like a bird in a cage that won't let a probing finger go unpunished.

For me, John Brown was the only client there who scared me. Not physically, mind you, but emotionally. I was afraid to look at him. You know how that is, when a person is so deformed or so ugly or so misfigured that just a peek at him clouds your mind and sends tingles down your spine? That's how it was with him and me.

He'd sit in his chair, guarding his room, watching two people at the same time. His mind worked as well as could be expected. He vociferated about a few things, mostly about his mother, who I was told never came to visit him. He'd call out like a crow on a rooftop, just letting his flock know he was there—"I'm worried about my mother! I'm worried about my mother! I'm worried about my mother!" His head would lean back slightly as he said this. And always in threes the lines came out. Then, after the three lines were cawed, he'd go back to his watching and guarding. If you happened to stray close to him he might say something like: "This is my shirt, not your shirt.

This is my shirt, not your shirt. This is my shirt, not your shirt." You got used to this after a while so that when he cawed you wouldn't hear him, it'd go in one ear and out the other, so to speak, and you'd have to ask yourself constantly, "Did John Brown just call out or was I imagining that he did?"

I didn't deal much with him. Dorothy seemed to be able to work best with him. If he had a stained shirt, which he often did, she'd make him change it. That was always a show to watch:

"John Brown you get in there and change that shirt!"

"I'm worried about my moth—"

"Oh, you leave yo' mother 'lone an' get in there an' change that shirt fo' I change it fo' you. Do you hear me?" She'd stand over him, invading his space, arms akimbo.

"This is my shirt not your shirt . . . " Then the battle would begin. Dorothy would start unbuttoning it and he'd try to stop her. And then he'd stand up and Dorothy, beautiful Dorothy, would wrestle him back into his room until finally he'd be there crying with no tears in his eyes, conceding, saying it was his shirt and not her shirt, and he was worried about his mother. But he was taking it off as Dorothy stood there, arms akimbo, breathing a little heavily.

Now John Brown had Progeria, the dreaded "Aging Disease," and I knew he was thirty-seven years old and so somehow, some way, I had reasoned myself into believing that yes, that body and that face had a thirty-seven-year-old quality to it, and if it weren't for the Progeria he'd look thirty-seven.

Things happened very unexpectedly around there so you had to be on your guard. It was like living in a three-dimensional surrealism. A person like Dorothy was used to it, but a newcomer like myself was vulnerable. I learned this very quickly.

Dorothy, on this particular day, had him take both his pants and his shirt off and she was madder than her usual equanimitous self because he had put up a good fight this time.

"Now you change that shirt and them pants and don't be givin' me no mo' fuss, John Brown."

Even he was out of breath today, which was a strange thing to see, him huffing and puffing like that. But because he was huffing and puffing his teeth were showing extra clearly and both Dorothy and I noticed them.

"John Brown, look at those teeth. OOOO WEEE they stained. You take them out right now and clean them," Dorothy ordered.

He was defeated and he couldn't fight anymore, and besides, he had no saying about his dentures being his, so he just reached right up there and grabbed his teeth and pulled them out of his head.

His face fell! I had never seen him without those things in his mouth. His face fell a good half a foot! I heard myself yelp or shout, and then I went running from the room, out into the lounge, in reflex from the sight. But I had seen it! He had shriveled in the wink of an eye. He had aged a half a century right in front of me. You see it on television, in horror films, in cartoons, but to see a real live person transform right in front of you like that, from a quasi forty-year-old to an octogenarian . . . you lose a piece of your mind.

On a Sunday afternoon about one month later with the weekend crew on, John Brown, sitting outside his room as usual, suddenly leaned his head back and crowed something peculiar: "I've got a heart attack in my stomach. I've got a heart attack in my stomach! I've got a heart attack in my stomach!"

He didn't appear any different than normal, didn't indicate he was in pain or show any outward signs of distress. Just sat there. So no one reacted to this utterance, not even the floor nurse, I was told. Ten minutes later he was dead.

herman boecker felt no pain

Cigarettes were king. Without cigarettes the ship would have sunk and all would have drowned. Nearly everyone smoked, even the most unlikely of characters. In fact, those who didn't smoke couldn't because of lung ailments or strict doctors' orders prohibiting them from the indulgence. They were a pitiable lot, the non-smokers. Cigarettes were everything—e.g., weapon, reward, friend, lover, mother. I was often assigned the duty of distributing those panaceas, and I must admit I rather enjoyed the job. It was power, pure and simple. Who held the cigarettes was idolized as much as any god past or present.

Since absolute power corrupts absolutely, I'd order everyone around and they'd acquiesce to my every whimsical command.

"Shirley, pick up that straw!"

"Margaret, help Mrs. Tyson out of her chair."

"Floyd, empty your pockets."

Etc.

Herman Boecker was one of our three Alzheimer's patients, and other than John Brown, they were, all three of them, the worst off. Herman was only about forty-five and had been a lawyer with a wife and kids, five kids to be exact. Had his own private practice, a well-known name throughout the state. He was a brilliant man, a merit scholar, active in politics, a do-gooder in the community, a musician—played the saxophone in a jazz band. In his room, above his bed, his wife had placed a framed picture of him shaking hands with JFK back when Herman was a student at Johns Hopkins. His wife no longer came to visit. It was much too taxing on the poor woman. Dorothy said she sold everything, packed up and moved to Oregon to start a new life. It was the best thing she could do; I mean she was still young, and there was really nothing left of her husband anymore.

To describe Herman physically is easy because he was a zombie. His eyes stared blankly ahead, his mouth hung open partly, and his wrists curled down pulling his hands under them. He would sit all day as described, getting up every forty-five minutes to collect his two cigarettes when reissuement time came. What was unbelievable about Herman was that his brain, or a part of it anyway, worked perfectly well. They say they can't remember from one minute to the next, but that man could talk, even if he did mumble incomprehensibly at times causing you to get up close to his face in order to hear what he was saying. He was still cognizant, there was no denying that.

I had a conversation with him once. A rather lengthy conversation at that. It was Paul, the floor nurse, who told me that his brain still worked and that he could talk about any subject except, of course, what he had eaten for lunch the day before. I'd always been interested in becoming a gentleman farmer, and when Paul told me that Herman had, in fact, been a gentleman farmer, well, I had to employ him as an interlocutor. . . .

"Say, Herman?"

"Um myes?" He mumbled and rocked forward when he spoke. He always, I noticed, started his sentences with an "Um."

"I hear you had a farm."

"Um, myes, mthats mright."

"Well, I've always thought about having a farm one day. What kind of animal do you think is the best to make money on? Chickens, pigs, sheep, cows?"

"Um, mpigs mare mbest. Um mthey mgain mweight mfast, myou mcan mfeed mthem mquite mcheaply, mand myou mget ma mgood mprice mper mpound."

"What about chickens?"

"Um, mthey're mbetter mfor myour mown mtable. Um, mselling mthem mis mhard mwork mand mthey're mnot mas mbig mas ma mpig mso myou mdon't mmake mas mmuch mper mpound." A font of information he was. Every question I asked he answered so informatively and concisely. He'd never offer a comment, however, he'd only respond to a question, unless of course you were holding the cigarettes, in which case he'd ask you for one every two minutes. Yes, besides the zombieness and his smell—I'll get to that—he was perfectly aware . . . or so it seemed.

Herman was a good sport. He did everything himself, but he couldn't shave on account of his wrists. And for some reason, he stank. I don't know why this was. He'd shower after breakfast and by dinner time he'd be reeking like week-old carrion.

He liked his cigarettes, that man, and he was one of the most zealous command takers if a cigarette was in it for him.

I had reissued the cigarettes a good ten minutes before and I was sitting imperiously playing a game of cards with Merry Mary when I noticed a funky burning smell. Paul was there too, and we both had our noses in the air sniffing.

"Something's burning," I said to him.

"I smell it," he acknowledged.

I got up and looked all around, under the tables, in the waste baskets, in between the cushions of the chairs. Nothing. Yet the pungent odor grew more offensive. Paul and I looked at one another with arched brows.

I took one more look around and couldn't find anything.

Suddenly I realized something—I was standing next to Herman Boecker who was sitting zombielike as usual and he was the only one still smoking. That funky, burning odor was coming off of him. I took a step closer to him when I saw it and let out a wail—

"HERMAN! THE CIGARETTE!"

He rocked forward to look at his cigarette because he would move his body before he'd move his hands, and he let out a howl like a harpooned seal. He rocked to his feet and began desperately to wave his hand back and forth, but the cigarette held fast—it was stuck good and proper, burnt right into the flesh.

I panicked. I jerked my head from side to side, looking for a towel, a cloth, anything, turning and twisting in my spot. Finally, I just ripped the shirt off of my back, wrapped it around my hand and grabbed that cigarette roach of his and pulled it from the flesh. Paul said something stupid I remember—

"That's it, no more filterless cigarettes."

My stomach was in knots. I examined Herman. He was excited about it all, his eyes were wide open, even wider open than their usual wide open selves. His finger was all black and brown, charred clear to the bone. And boy did it smell, the whole room smelled. But then a ghastly realization came over me. He felt no pain!

I studied that face for signs of a cringe, a grimace, or even an "Ouch." Nothing. He hadn't felt a thing, not even a tickle.

Alzheimer's . . . the great white shark in the sea of mental illness. No pills or programs to defend against that beast, just a nice secure tank to keep him in so the rest of us can live in peace.

makin' beds

Kelvin and I were cut from the same slab of cosmic plasma. We looked nothing alike, spoke an almost incompatible dialect of the same language, enjoyed different pleasures, and so on. But those were all the superficialities of our conditioning. Deep down we were the same. Kelvin and I were dreamers. We both had fanciful visions of a bigger better us. He would one day win the lottery, buy a couple of car dealerships, and spend his life wheeling and dealing and "livin' large." And I, on the other side of happiness, would travel the world, write a book, a good book, and be a scion of the great Russian literary tradition. We were as like as twins, which is why we worked so well together.

In the meantime, that is, while Kelvin and I waited for our ships to come in, we wiped assholes for a living, tied people to chairs, played mind games with paranoids, shaved faces, made beds. This latter job was, I must confess, my number one favorite. All my life I had hated making my bed—saw no real purpose in it. Kelvin changed all that. He glorified the chore, made its subtle import come alive with each tug of the sheet. A well-made bed, in my book now, is next to godliness.

About an hour after breakfast we made beds together for forty-five minutes. We'd make fifteen beds in that time, distractions included. God we were good. The air would bristle as we laid into those cotton sheets and blankets and bedspreads. We were attractive to the eye, too. Many's the time, I recall, when people, strangers to the facility, stood in the doorway watching us make those beds. They saw the singularity in our purpose, the skill and pride in the way we manipulated those sheets. I believe that we could have put those fifteen beds on stage and entertained the hell out of an audience for every second of that forty-five minutes. I believe it still.

We hardly ever spoke. We didn't have to. Megs would come with us, and even he sat and watched us admiringly, room after room, sitting there with that dumb, peaceful look on his puss as the billowing sheets snapped, crackled, and popped all around him.

"The grip the thang, Rich," Kelvin taught me that first day. "You grab da sheet in the righ' spot and you jus' needs ta tug a little." This he said as he worked and demonstrated. That day I watched him make every bed but the last two. Then it was my turn. He scrutinized my every movement.

"No, no, Rich, yo' feet walkin' too much. I make da bed in ten ste's. You fine yo' place an' stay there. Righ' side, lef' side, it don' matter, you jus' needs to change sides fo' da co'nahs an' da tuck.

"Let the air straighten da sheet. You ain' a eyeron—swish swish wid yo' han's. Let the air smooth them out. When you opens it up, tug quick fo' she hit da mattress.

"Now there ain' no reason fo' you movin' a bed. Don' shake yo' head, I saw you move it. No reason to move a bed, 'less maybe we in John Brown's room where he gots his over close to da wall. Sometime you need to bump it back a inch o' two.

"You holdin' da sheet too far from da en' fo' yo' co'nah. Shouldn't be no more'n a foot. Tight, you wan' everthang tight an' sharp for these people. Le' them loose it up, they have no problem wid dat. You see these beds da mo'nin' after, they good an' loose.

"The bedspread de icin'. But it don' look no good 'less da cake smooth un'erneath.

"Where da spread fold un'er the pillow should look like a woman's cleavage—make you wanna run yo' finger up in there.

"Now dat ain' bad. Po'tential here, po'tential."

In two weeks time I was his equal. In fact, at times, I felt I surpassed him, especially on the cleavages, but it was pure vanity on my part to entertain such a notion.

I hope I die in a well-made bed.

touch me touch you

"Who the hell is that?"

"That tudge me tudge you. You never seen him befo'?"

"No."

"He up early ev'yday, and out befo' breakfas'. Don' usually come back 'til supper. He got a full bag 'ats why. He got the walkin' privilege." Kelvin and I stood in the doorway of Capn' John's room watching this bent over little man shaped like a lower case "r" digging furiously inside a fully stuffed trash bag. "Tudge 'im."

"I'm not going to touch him," I frowned.

"Go 'head, he don' bite cha. Tudge 'im."

So I touched him and he touched me back almost unconsciously. He didn't acknowledge me or my presumptuousness in the least. "What's that all about?" I asked as if it had some special significance.

"He jus' always tudge you back. He got a thang 'bout it."

"How do you know this?"

"It jus' the way it is. You tudge him he gonna tudge you back."

"Yeah, well what if you don't want to be touched back?" I felt rather peevish on this day, I recall.

"He tudge you back, mayn, that's all I gonna say 'bout it." Kelvin started walking out of the room, and I grabbed him.

"Wait a minute, you can't tell me you haven't tried touching him and then not letting him touch you back."

"Yeah, I tried that."

"Well?"

"He always tudge ya back, that's all there is to it."

"Oh yeah?" Not having any of it, I marched into the room and flicked my jab out and touched the man on the shoulder, turned, and sprinted out the door.

He took off after me like I had just stolen his first-born child. It was a frightening sight, seeing that little leprechaun sprinting down the hall after me, his eyes wild as a lassooed mare. He could run, too. Afraid that he might hurt himself, or that the administration would see me running away from this paranoid, I quit and let him touch me.

Touch Me Touch You was an enigma from the word go. There was almost nothing in his file about his previous life. No siblings, no parents or relatives of any kind. Apparently he had been an orphan and a transient for most of his life. According to his records, he was born in Colorado to a woman with an Irish name. No father mentioned. The only history described in his charts dated back to the late forties when he worked for several years in a coal mine in West Virginia, which might explain his posture. After that it's assumed he'd just always lived on the street, and only through the benevolent intervention of the state was it possible for him to finally take up "permanent" residence in the twilight of his life. But old habits die hard, and nary a day did he miss out on the street, rummaging through dumpsters and filling his plastic bag with sundries.

As puerile as it may sound, I always harbored the great notion to one day touch him on my way out of work, and then run home. I remember telling Kelvin of this idea.

"Go 'head, try it," he frowned. Kelvin, as big a gamester as he was, always had a tone of futility in his voice whenever I broached the subject of touching the little guy.

"You think he'd chase me home? C'mon, it's a mile at least to my apartment."

"Like I say, go 'head, try it."

"Have you tried it?"

"Don' matter what I done."

"Seriously, you think he'd chase me?"

"I awready tole you once: you tudge him, he tudge you back."

"Right away or will he wait? Now there's a question for you."

"Jus' as soon as he cain, jus' as soon as he cain."

My chance came when I least expected it. I was out walking the streets late at night some months later when I spotted him gleaning through a dumpster behind a grocery store ten blocks from my place. He was totally unaware of me. I got a good running start, and "smack," I hit him on the butt and didn't stop running nor did I look back 'til I was up in my apartment behind a locked door. I remember beaming with childish pride, thinking about how I would call up Kelvin and brag.

That night I tossed and turned and couldn't seem to get to sleep. I remember feeling very edgy and expectant, as if something untoward was going to happen. Finally, as sleepless nights always go for me, I managed to fall into peaceful slumber just before daybreak. Then in the midst of a tranquil dream, I felt it—a spine-tingling tap on my foot. I woke up with a start, my toes still buzzing from the contact, just in time to hear my apartment door close with a click.

I never touched him again.

There are many things that would be better left untouched in this world. In fact, I think that's the fundamental difference between the black race and the white race—the black race understands this basic law of nature; the white race does not.

the walk

I hadn't been there but a month when the thought occurred to me that the entire community of them needed some fresh air.

The second "walk" idea of mine was a greater, more thorough flop than my first, although eons shorter. I just remember that I saw the sun shining brilliantly outside, its bold rays glistening off the thermometer beyond the day room's big window, the blood red mercury reading a calid sixty-eight degrees. That was enough for me:

"Let's take them outside for a walk!" I burst out.

"Outside? Rich, they cayn't do no walkin'. Where we gonna takes them anyway?" Kelvin asked, his thick eyebrows bent steeply over his wide eyes.

"Just down to the lakefront and back. It's not far."

He shook his head definitively—"The fron' too far!"—case closed.

"It is not. It's just across the street for godsake. Shit, they walk around here twice as far as that every day. Look at Sweetie Pie."

"She the only one."

"What about Megs, and Leslie, Ole Jake and even Herman?"

"Doubt dat."

"Shirley's strong too, she could do it."

"She ain' the type take a walk, Rich."

"Well, none of them are. But fuck, it's so nice outside, let's just take them out on the sidewalk. They've probably been inside for months," I argued, as the probable truth that nary a one had ever stepped out into the light of day since coming to the place pinched me hard. That same thought pinched Kelvin too.

"Gots to get 'proval," Kelvin challenged, reminding me of that endall of life. For Kelvin, the system, the mechanism called society, was soundly edified to dissuade against such whimsy. And as a black man, he realized this intrinsically, as well he should. But black whimsy and white whimsy are altogether different beasts, albeit both capable of great destruction and ado. Moreover, the edifice was in place for the very purpose of defending against black whimsy; always has been. However, with white whimsy like mine, there was no edifice in place, only censure. Big deal! For me, censure, like failure, has always been an inspiration.

The Great Walk idea was greeted with open-minded interest, surprisingly, by the powers that be. They nodded as I gave a detailed description, and rubbed their chins upon the conclusion of my proposal. Yes, a meritorious notion for sure, but who and where. Kelvin and I had compiled a list and handed it immediately over to Gloria. They studied it, Gloria and Big Bird, murmured together, and surprisingly handed it back with a stamp of approval, crossing off the names of Leslie, Mon Cherie, and Herman. Kelvin and I were stunned. We did not expect to get such resounding support. We stood for a moment staring at each other unsure of what our next move was to be.

"Let's go!" I encouraged him with a clap on the shoulder. "We should be back in an hour or two," I said walking away.

"Take your time. Let them enjoy the air," Big Bird gleamed. In retrospect, that gleam of hers should have been forewarning, for in my mind's eye I see that twisted smile so clearly now—

evil, prescient, witch-like. But at the time I was blind to it. I was caught up in the inspiration of The Walk.

With our motley crew, we broke out into the light of day. There were ten of us, including Kelvin and me. Our goal was the small traffic island park about 300 yards north, with its green benchs, rhododendrons, and a half-dozen human-high trees wired to the ground and fenced off to keep the dogs from pissing on them. From there we would assess the troops to see if they had the wherewithal to walk the additional 400 yards farther to the lakefront, keeping in mind, of course, the return jaunt as well. If we deemed them unfit at any point, we had decided that we would retreat to the Rainbow post haste. This was our peripatetic plan.

When the lepers marched through town a millenium ago, the lead leper would ring a loud bell to warn those on the road or in the town ahead of the loathsome group's imminent passage. The unexpected sound of that leper's bell must have borne with it the most chilling and yet the most delicious tone. The townspeople no doubt fled like cockroaches at the first clang, but once safely behind closed doors, the window curtains at the bottom corners would most certainly have been pulled away revealing shiny, expectant eyeballs greedily awaiting the goulish sight. In our case, we had no bell ringer at the lead, and even if we did it would have done us no good because the vast majority of our admirers were hermetically sealed inside their cars. Expressions ranged the whole gamut of physiognomy, from utter terror, to sublime hilarity.

Cars slowed, people stared in open-mouthed awe. Those unfortunate souls who happened to be on the same sidewalk and walking towards us, were confronted with a shocking gauntlet that paralyzed them. In each case, the pedestrian stood to one side of the sidewalk and waited with eyes downcast for us to pass by. I must say myself, we were truly a magnificent sight. Led by Kelvin all dressed in white with Megs in tow, the most exquisite file of Curly and Shirley and Bob White and Ole Jake,

Bobby, Sweetie Pie, Cap'n John, and me. We could have paraded through the circus at center ring and gotten a good round of applause wearing the self-same outfits.

The march to the island park midway between the lake and the Rainbow was suspiciously easy. The entire jaunt was accomplished in about five minutes time. No one was guilty of any untoward action, other than Bob White's insistence on pointing out his shoes and pants to every innocent bystander he passed. If we were leading men into battle, Kelvin and I, we would have led them all right into an ambush!

"Hey, you was right, Rich. No problem," Kelvin said as soon as we had arrived at the park and were lounging on the green benches.

"Yeah, it was easier than I thought," I agreed.

"We takes them to the beach, no question," he said with a smile and a deep breath, glancing back at the Rainbow, still visible from our position, then eyeballing the proposed route down the inclined lane, across the field and street to the beach. While all the clients sat apathetically like herd animals unknowing of why they were at rest or where they were headed, Kelvin and I both quietly indulged ourselves in interior boastings. I know my head was full of soliloquy, and his being just a few feet from me, I could almost hear his mind's recitatives bouncing out phrases in iambic pentameter. We were proud of ourselves and our mission, as well we should have been. And that great respite between the Rainbow and the deep blue sea afforded us such delightful revery. That was to be the highlight of the peregrination.

"Let's move 'em out," Kelvin commanded.

Without the slightest hesitation, we roused the troops and headed for the beach—Kelvin at the lead and I in the rear. What made it so beguiling was the slight declivity. From the island park to the lake front it was downhill, of a grade as precipitous as that of a movie theater. For us it was like an elevator. We coasted down and down and down with ease. At the bottom it was a mere 150-yard cruise across a flat playing field, then thirty yards across Lakefront Avenue to the beach. A piece of cake. We paused there at the edge of the field.

To the well-trained eye of a field sergeant, the first signs of trouble no doubt would have been detected at this point. A good look into the eyes of the troops would have revealed a repetitive sentiment of vertigo, fatigue, and low morale. Neither Kelvin or I detected even the slightest negative vibrations.

"Jus' 'bout there," Kelvin beamed, his nostrils flaring out wide with youth and nobility. He looked over us all like a proud papa, standing tall, Megs leaning extra hard on his arm. "Now listen ev'ybody, we goin' cross dis fiel', an' when we gets to dat beach, we gonna sit oursel's down in da san'. Be nice day fo' sittin' on da beach. Take yo' shoes off. Run da san' through yo' toes." It was a beautiful image he painted, but I don't think a one of them was impressed by it. Just me.

We never made it to the beach. The 150-yard playing field was in reality a poisoned field of poppies; under that not so friendly sun, that field took away our legs, our hearts, our will.

"Ahn hahn hahn hahn . . . " Bobby's cry was the harbinger of doom. Not even thirty yards onto the field he began to break down.

"Wha's matter widchu, boy?" Kevlin crowed playfully, not even bothering to turn around to look at him.

"Boy, ahn hahn hahn hahn hahn . . . " The crying became more desperate.

Kelvin turned around fiercely. "Now you cut it out, you ruin' da fun fo' ev'ybody!"

"Body, hahn hahn hahn hahn hahn hahn . . . ." The crying persisted.

Finally, about halfway across the field Kelvin stopped the march and moved back to Bobby, having an unusually difficult time with Megs on his arm, practically having to carry him.

"You always bein' da baby," Kelvin jawed at Bobby, two inches from his nose.

"Bay—by, ahn hahn hahn ha—"

Then Curly fainted. He went down like a sack of potatoes falling off a counter.

"Shit!" I cried.

"They fallin' out!" Kelvin turned violently to see ashen Curly, eyes slammed shut, lying in a heap on the cool October grass, face as white as snow. I hopped from my spot behind Cap'n John's wheelchair and knelt down over Curly.

In the space of time that it took both Kelvin and I to get him to a seated position and conscious, Bob White had wandered off almost back to the edge of the field. Meanwhile, Bobby and Ole Jake had plopped themselves down on the field. Bobby was lying supine trying to find a comfortable position in which to sleep. Then Shirley and Sweetie Pie got into a row. Fists began to fly, along with invectives.

"Rich, get Bob White!" Kelvin commanded as he jumped to his feet and raced into the frightening female fray.

I did as I was told and raced over to catch Bob White, yelling for him to stop with each stride. By the time I reached him, he had made it halfway up the incline, wandering along at an un-hurried gait. I grabbed hold of his shirt sleeve and tugged.

"Whoa there, Hoss!"

"Look, shoes! Shoes!" he pointed. I looked down hypnot-ically. "Look!" Then his finger pointed out perpendicularly, down at the group in the middle of the field. My eye followed. What I saw shocked me and to this day I can see it all just as clearly in my mind's eye as I did with my own two then. It looked like a disaster area, like an airplane crash or something. From our perspective, some seventy-five yards away and up about ten feet, we witnessed the mayhem—bodies strewn about the ground randomly while in the middle stood Kelvin

and a teetering Megs between two witches who were yelling
and screaming the most vile curses at one another, barely audi-
ble from up there.

Again, hindsight is 20/20 vision, and what I should have
done at that point was to take Bob White immediately back to
the roost and gotten help. Instead, the moment I saw Kelvin
put both his hands to his face I charged back down to the flock,
practically dragging Bob White behind me. In her anxiety to
get at Shirley, Sweetie Pie had inadvertently poked Kelvin in
the eye. She got him good. It was disturbing because having
known Kelvin as I did, for him to be injured by a client was so
unusual, he was always so nimble and quick, forever dancing his
way gracefully out of harm's way. However, given the circum-
stances, it was understandable.

By the time I arrived he was doubled over swearing to high
heaven. At least Sweetie Pie and Shirley had ceased their skir-
mishing.

"Look at that son of a bitch!" Shirley had her wrath trained
on Kelvin now instead of Sweetie Pie. "He's not so tough.
Fuckin' nigger! Why don't you start to cry?"

"Wha wha what's the matter? Wha wha wha what is it,
honey?" Megs all disoriented without Kelvin to hold onto, was
shuffling around in a circle, frantically, like a dog barking at the
strangeness around him.

It was at that point that I remember thinking of the scene
from *The Wizard of Oz*—the scarecrow and the tin man realizing under the watchful glass orb of the wicked witch that she
must have put them under a spell. I had supplanted, of course,
Gloria's visage for that of the Wicked Witch of the West's. I
could see her twitching, little mousy nose pressed close to
the glass ball, stroking it with her stubby fingers. And there
we lay, Kelvin bent over, Megs shuffling around in a circle barking, Sweetie Pie looking down on him, Shirley growling, Curly
and Bobby and Ole Jake strewn about on the grass, Cap'n John

and Bob White and I just there looking stupid. I wanted to yell for help.

Apropos of looking to the street for assistance, a crowded carload of swarthy males was at that very moment slowly cruising up the incline behind us, their beat-up and jacked-up jalopy pounding out a menacing beat with an inky cloud of blue smoke hovering behind it. There were bare arms visible, hanging from the windows gesticulating in our direction.

"Fuckin' Puerto Ricans! Fuckin' Puerto Ricans!" Shirley, who had an almost full-time case of Tourette's, suddenly exploded with venomous song from behind me. The car slowed to a crawl. The arms stopped gesticulating. Shirley, true to her junkyard dog mentality, began to walk quickly toward the car, keeping up her rhythmic imprecations—"Fuckin' Puerto Ricans! Fuckin' Puerto Ricans! Fuckin' Puerto Ricans . . ." I abandoned Bob White and ran after her. I grabbed her and yanked her around. We stood face to face. She was a tall woman, close to six feet, so she was actually looking down at me. I heard a shout. I turned to see the car at rest at the end of the field. "Fuckin' Puerto Ricans! Fuckin'—" I instinctively put my hand up to her mouth and promptly got it bit.

"OW! SHIT!" I jerked my hand away waving it vigorously, the pain surging in spurts through my entire body. At that moment, out of the corner of my eye, I saw a familiar color moving toward the pounding car. It was Bob White. Pain clouding my head, I staggered after him, catching him by the collar. "No! Get back! Stay here!"

"You stupid fuckin' cretin, where are you gonna go? As if you know, you fuckin' Down's syndrome case!" Shirley never missed an insult. My hand, the palm of my hand, hurt like hell. Again, the image of Gloria ogling at us through her glass ball flooded my head with rage. The disaster was in full effect. There seemed no way out. Even the carload of swarthies wanted no part of our dilemma and sputtered off, blowing a toxic blue cloud up into the sky for good measure.

With Bob White and Shirley in tow, I stood over the dazed circle of defectives. We all stood there stupefied, watching Kelvin work on his eye, like a ship's crew waiting for the ineluctable foundering of its vessel, the captain in the middle saying prayers.

When he had restored himself somewhat, his eye shut tight and swollen, he stood up tall and took a long assessing look around with his one open eye. Even in the one eye you could read the entire situation like a movie screen—"Fucked Up!"

"Should I run back and get someone at the place to help?" I suggested.

"No mayn, they fire us bof we makes the place look bad."

"Yeah, but, but how're we gonna get 'em all back there? Bobby, Ole Jake, Megs, Curly, they're not going to make it. I could just quickly run up there and get someone."

"Who you gonna get that gonna help dis? If we cayn's do it oursel's, ain' no one else gonna do it fo' us. Beside, we be fire fo' sho." He winced as he spoke; you could feel his pain and anger as he stood there all proud and determined. However, that pain and anger and determination was no match for the dysfunction which existed around us. So there we stood, one black male, twenty-five, dressed in white with one functioning eye, one white male, twenty-three, also in white with a throbbing palm, and eight dysfunctional, schizophrenic, senile idiots in myriad colors waiting for a hand to reach down to make the next move.

"Git up, boy!" Kelvin broke the revery with a growl at Bobby.

"Up boy ahn hahn hahn hahn . . . " He didn't move. I could tell that Kelvin had an overwhelming urge to plant a field goal sized kick to his ribs. And even if he had, Bobby wouldn't have moved from that spot. Curly and Ole Jake were roustable, but how far they could be prodded to ambulate was questionable. And all the while like a wind-up toy, Bob White was yearning under my grasp to wander off.

A dozen different scenarios played through our heads. And it was Kelvin who voiced the very idea that my mind kept turning a circle around:

"We put Bobby in Cap'n John's chair. One of us carry Cap'n John jus' up to the park."

There was no protest. That was one positive in our favor, like Sisyphus's rock that had to be rolled to the top of the hill, whatever we wanted to try, there would be no argument. I shouldn't say no protest, Cap'n John did grumble a little bit, but when I assured him there was a cigarette in it for him—dangling the white spike in front of him—he shut up immediately. I yanked him from the seat and placed him on the pallid green grass like a bag of groceries, placing the cigarette between his lips and lighting it for him. He sat or stood, I'm not sure which term is right when describing a legless man on the ground, puffing that white stick joyously, looking up at us as if he were casually sinking into the earth, content with his fate.

"Oh mayn you shit yo'self. You did dat on purpose!" I swear it was at that point that Kelvin's black face actually had a shade of red to it. We loaded stinking Bobby into Cap'n John's chair with a vengeance. The shit was oozing through his trousers.

"Maybe I should run up there and get Dorothy or someone now," I suggested stupidly. "Take me five minutes."

"Rich, you dissin' me wit dat." Kelvin was adamant.

With Megs in place under his arm, Kelvin began to push Bobby back across the field, walking proudly like a mother duck confident that her ducklings were in hot pursuit. But the rest of the group just lay there on the grass looking after the three.

"Come on! Get up!" he turned and yelled, glaring at us all. That seemed to do it, as Ole Jake and Curly slowly got to their feet. I had to let go of Shirley and Bob White to pick up Cap'n John, which caused me some hestitation. It had to be done.

Cap'n John was light, and I hoisted him over my shoulder like a continental soldier.

Kelvin, determined to make it off the field, actually did, but the rest of us never made it. Within fifty paces, Shirley and Sweetie Pie got into it again. As if it had been a pattern for years, Ole Jake and Curly both sat down on the grass as soon as the fireworks began.

"'Moke, 'moke, give me a puff!" Cap'n John cockle-doodle-dooed in my ear. I quickly placed him down on the grass again and stuck a butt between his lips and lit it. I admired him for being so easily placated. Before I had the least inclination, Kelvin leaped into the middle of the ladies' fray and pushed Shirley to the ground hard, no doubt getting his vengeance for her earlier epithet. But pushing her down like that was the wrong thing to do! It just made her angrier. She vaulted to her feet and flew at Sweetie Pie hell-bent on murder. It was all the both of us could do to keep the two apart, getting dinged in the process. The Furies couldn't hold a flame to those two.

Within five minutes there were three cop cars parked on the street, their hysteria lights defaming the sunlight around us, and six cops sorting through the mayhem. In the report, which I had a glimpse at later, a passerby's account of this vicious brawl between Sweetie Pie and Shirley was what had alerted the men in blue. All six officers, I remember, were rather stoic about the whole thing and suspicious of intent and motivation as are all cops, much to their discredit.

We were all driven back to the Rainbow by the police, all except Bob White, Kelvin and Cap'n John. Bob White had wandered off even before the police had arrived and was found an hour later at a convenience store smelling to high heaven of excrement. Kelvin had insisted on pushing Cap'n John home himself, refusing to admit defeat and ride in the cop car. I remember looking back at him through the rear window of the cruiser and recognizing the pride and defiance in his gait. I truly admired his spirit, his pugnacity; and in retrospect I realize his determination to get the group back safely without help was for the clients' sake, not his own pride. Up until that point, now I know, the administration had had virtually nothing on any of those people, nothing that could have been construed as evidence in support of their transferals. But the horrors of the Great Walk offered proof, documented by the police yet. Sweetie Pie and Shirley were made most vulnerable and all the others likewise received the black mark. Kelvin knew that, that's why he fought so valiantly until the bitter end. In fact, I had mentioned a few days later that we should have gotten help.

"Don' ya un'erstan' Rich, mayn, dat de las' thing we shoulda done," he said, wagging his finger at me.

He was absolutely right, it was all or nothing. Anyway, the idea was mine, and I took full responsibility for all as I tried desperately to convince Gloria and Big Bird. They only smiled goulishly, patronizingly, and told me not to worry, that it was nobody's fault and all was fine as no one was hurt by the experience.

There's nothing quite so unsettling as words of comfort from your enemies.

kelvin and fred

Fred was a paranoid. He slept like a bear in hybernation, every-day, all day long. He was irascible, especially with "the mens" as Dorothy would say. In fact, Dorothy was the only one who could make him laugh. She'd stroke him with a word or two—"Fred, honey, you look gooood today," she'd say in that black southern gal tone, and he'd purr and giggle like a child. But with us, with Kelvin and me, he'd glower and growl like a junk-yard dog.

Fred was Kelvin's nemesis. Tall, lithe, fast-handed, smooth talking, insightful Kelvin had all "the mens" figured out. Of course he had his occasional problems with one or the other, but Fred was a daily competition. We, as a matter of fact, started the day out with Fred.

Fred, by the way, wasn't his real name. He was a Ukranian, Fyodor Markolovich . . . something like that. Ironically, he looked exactly like an aging, balding version of the cartoon character, Fred Flintstone—same gruff voice and disposition. This likeness, however, had nothing to do with his being called Fred; they gave him the name simply because it was easier to say. Fred had been a mason in his former life. He had had a wife, but she had died years before. There were no children, and only one living brother who resided in California. No, Fred was alone, which is how he liked it, I'm sure. Fred just wanted to sleep the rest of his life away. At times I found myself sympathetic to that aspiration, contrary to Nick the Barber's philosophy of life.

I'm convinced that Fred kept Kelvin coming back to his job year after year. By the time I had arrived on the scene, Kelvin had been at Fred for going on six years. And I'm also convinced that it was Kelvin who kept Fred from lapsing into catalepsy. In a way it was a symbiotic relationship in that Kelvin kept his job and his family fed, and Fred remained alive and somewhat or marginally functional.

Kelvin would bound into the room with a towel curled around his neck giving him the aspect of a linebacker wearing a neck brace. I'd close the thick oak door behind us, privatizing the proceedings. Fred would be snoring, his nude body turned buttside out toward both of us at the far end of the room. Kelvin would flip on the radio next to his bed—loud, very loud. Fred would not be in the least bit disturbed by the racket. Kelvin would find his insolent rap station and then he'd set up shop. I had my duties, too. Fred's roommate, Megs, was an eighty-year-old ex-boxer with the "Old Timer's" disease. Megs was Kelvin's main charge during the day because he'd punch people if you didn't monitor him closely. Anyway, at five feet four inches, Megs was fairly docile and easy to manage in the morning, you just couldn't put your face too close to his or he'd whack you one. In ten minutes I'd have him dressed and ready to go. After that, Megs and I would sit back and watch the show.

Kelvin would get a pan of hot water with a washcloth for shaving. He'd line up his razor and shaving cream and chucks and underwear and clothes on Fred's dresser. Then he'd sit on Fred's bed with him and begin playing a lilting beat on Fred's corpulent backside. Kelvin was quite a drummer. The slapping of hands on the white, flaccid flesh would ring throughout the room, growing more and more urgent as Kelvin's blurring hands hastened the beat. It would take ten seconds or more before you'd hear the low moan that would start as a simple "Ow" and grow and grow and grow until it was a thunderous "OW! OW! OW! YOU COCKSUCKING NIGGER BASTARD!" at which point Fred would begin to sit up, his eyes wide as saucers, his mouth bent with a murderous twist.

"Fred, honey, don't talk to your cousin that way," Kelvin would taunt him.

"I ain't your fuckin' cousin," Fred would rumble.

"Aw, sho we is. We gots the same gramma. We even looks alike, don' we Rich?" drawing me into it.

"You're nuts," Fred would say, smacking his lips and scratching himself as he followed his nemesis/savior with his big Bambi eyes. Kelvin would adeptly, at this point, slam an undershirt over Fred's head faster than the eye could see. This is what I always loved because it worked everytime—Kelvin would slam that T-shirt down over Fred's bald head, yank his arms through the sleeves, pull the front down, and with amazing celerity play the fastest barehanded drum roll you ever heard on the top of Fred's shiny dome. This would infuriate him so much that he would begin to rise hell-bent on murder. One thing I forgot to point out is that Fred was "the slowest movin' boday on earth," as Dorothy would say. Kelvin always had plenty of time to dodge Fred's fist or a grasping hand. He'd rise slowly, just as planned, and—budabing, budaboom, Kelvin would slap two chucks over his sleepy penis and buttocks, hold them in place with one hand, push poor Fred over backwards with the other hand, and as he fell back on the bed, his feet would come up off the floor giving Kelvin just enough time to get his size forty-four boxer shorts and load them in over his feet and knees. Another drumroll on the head; a cursing, snarling, and rising Fred; and whoosh—up came the shorts and Kelvin would have Fred's underwear on.

Next was shaving.

"Get your fucking hands off me, nigger," Fred would roar.

"Freddy, cousin, that's no way to talk to yo' kin."

"I ain't your cocksuckin' cousin."

"What would gramma say?"

Here Kelvin would allow Fred to grab one arm with both hands and try to break it while Kelvin, with the free arm, would apply the shaving cream. Sometimes, however, Fred would not cooperate exactly and he'd let go of Kelvin's arm and try grabbing something else just as Kelvin was applying the cream. In the ensuing struggle, Fred's entire head would be smeared with shaving cream much to my amusement. But Kelvin knew what Fred was capable of and rarely would he complain of Fred's hurting him at this juncture of the drama. Shaving cream in place, he'd wrestle his arm free and walk away for a moment. Invariably, the hybernating bear would begin to nod and within a minute's time he'd be sleeping sitting up, snoring with his head bent down so that his lathered chin rested against his T-shirted chest. Kelvin would spend this time helping me or mouthing the words and gesticulating to the rap music or counting his money. Eventually, he would return to Fred and quietly and happily shave his face. Fred would rarely awaken.

Most of the time, with the softness of an angel, Kelvin would be able to get him dressed; that is, he'd put on a shirt and button it all the way, pants he pulled up to Fred's knees, and the slippers he'd slide gently over Fred's gnarled feet. So Kelvin would shave him all up and gently wash the soap from his face and there he'd sit, his nutant form snoring peacefully, his pants hung around his knees. I remember one time Kelvin stepping back and looking down at Fred and asking me to do the same.

"Looky that mayn. He ain' crazy, he jus' lazy. Got hisself a warm bed, three meal a day, a nigger to shave his face an dress him up ev'yday. He ain' crazy, he jus' lazy. I tell you what crazy be. Crazy be havin' three kids, a wife, an' comin' here to work fo' fo'-fi'ty an hour to be a nigger to all these sof' brains. Crazy gettin' up ev'yday an' comin' here an' doin' dis shit fo' goin' on six year. No, that mayn ain' the crazy one. He jus' lazy."

Lazy isn't the word, Fred hated movement of any kind. He especially hated walking. If he could have had his druthers, he'd have readily accepted being wheelchaired around, from bed to dining table, to bath and back again. But this wasn't possible. We had to force walk him. The force walking was the ultimate competition.

After the shave and a playing of a happy beat on Fred's head, Fred would rise menacingly as usual and Kelvin would yank his pants in place and then the real battle would begin. Kelvin would put his nose up to Fred's and stare into his eyes balefully. Fred, like any good paranoid, hated to be stared at.

"What're you lookin' at you . . . you . . . nigger."

"You. You're ugly. OOO WEE! An you stanky, too."

"Look who's talkin'." Fred would retort and start getting ideas of sitting back down, even as provoked as he was.

"I'll bet yo' momma was ugly like you," Kelvin would say.

Fred's glower would deepen, making him forget about his comfort and he'd clench his fist and maybe even take a step toward Kelvin.

"You son of a bitch!" he'd grumble.

"But yo' gramma was pretty cause we cousins, remember?"

"Fuck you nigger!"

"You'd like that wouldn't you, Fredericka?" and Kelvin, playing a queer, would drape his arms over Fred's shoulders and bat his eyes at Fred. This always got Fred going and he'd try to hit Kelvin and he'd even walk after him for a couple of steps until he realized his dreaded predicament—he was standing in the middle of the floor miles from a place to sit down. In a panic, he'd look around himself, but like a lion onto a birthing wildebeast, Kelvin would pounce. He'd come around the back of Fred and cup his hands up into Fred's armpits and begin to half-push, half-carry him toward the door, barking orders at me as he went—"Move the chair!" "Get Megs outa the way!" "Open the door!"

What a rodeo it was! Fred, a good 250, and Kelvin a supple

and sinewy 160 at best, would be locked in battle like a cowboy with a bucking steer. Fred, with what little energy reserves he had, would try to extract himself from Kelvin's grasp while Kelvin remained steadfast on Fred's back like the skilled and powerful cowboy that he was. The duo rocked and zagged and cursed and gibed out the door and down the hall to the breakfast table . . .

"You cocksucking nigger bastard!" Fred bellowed.

"Now that ain' no way to talk to yo' cousin, cousin," Kelvin would reply.

beware the eyes of marge

Marge was 101 years old; she had her signed certificate from the president up on the wall to prove it. One of my favorite pastimes was to look up famous people in the back of my *Webster's* to see who was still alive when Marge was born: Van Gogh, Walt Whitman, Dostoyevsky, Tolstoy, Karl Marx, Ulysses S. Grant to name a few. Some guy named Chester Arthur was president at the time. Cars hadn't been invented and neither had planes, gorillas had yet to be discovered, Mt. Everest hadn't been climbed, Indians were hostile, the letting of blood was still practiced. In sum—Western civilization was in its infancy when Marge was born.

Marge was a tiny, moth-like creature who sat in a specially engineered chair in her doorway all day long. All you could see of Marge was her eyes, because she lay under reams and reams of sheets and blankets. Only Dorothy saw her body. Good thing.

"She such a delicate thang, Richud," Dorothy would say as I'd help her lift Marge and her miles of swaddling clothes gently out of her chair and into her bed some days after lunch. I remember I had a dream once about picking Marge up by myself. Marge was a moth underneath the sheets, with those blue bug eyes swirling and changing like a kaleidoscope, and all that fine pixie dust on her arms and legs sparkling. I, big oaf that I am, pawed her something terribly. I ruined her. She had big fingerprint marks all over her, and she was all frayed and quivery as she dragged herself off to a corner to die. Dreams . . .

But those eyes were uncanny. They were blue, fresco blue, all fuzzy and cloudy like gems from a millenium gone by. They saw and knew everything, those eyes. They had a crooked little smile to them, an omniscient smile. Those eyes knew it all— why the sun shined, the birds sang, the sky was blue. . . . They knew me, they knew Paul and Kelvin, they knew us through and through. And they knew exactly what was going on at the Rainbow Home, every profane bit of it.

You couldn't look too long or too directly at those eyes because they'd frighten you. There was too much knowledge and understanding in them. But if you happened to let your eyes wander and found yourself staring into them, they would never look away embarrassed or uninterested. They'd invite you in, seduce you, like the sirens they were. They were like having a bottomless pit two feet by two feet cut right in the middle of the floor with a fence around it. You could, if you wanted, stand on the edge and look down, but eventually your head would start to flutter and your stomach begin to spin.

For Kelvin, Marge was the opposite of Touch Me Touch You. Every morning at breakfast, Kelvin would touch Marge. I noticed this from the start and asked him about it.

"Gots to get me a piece a dat ev'yday. A hun'red an' one, mayn, tha's luck, pure an' simple. Tha' like tha' person survive the plane crash las' monf. Three hun'red dead an' only one survive. Put ten thousan' people together an' watch 'em go, only one gonna cross dat finish line a hun'red years later. Luck, mayn, gots to get me a piece a dat."

I liked the idea. So I started the ritual, touching Marge every day.

Marge didn't really belong there, or I shouldn't say that, she wasn't crazy like the others. But she'd always been there so in a sense she was the only one who truly belonged. She was left over from the days when the Rainbow Home used to be just an old folks home. An old folks home, decades ago, and there she still was, watching them all come and go, come and go. She had lived a normal life. Had a family, worked as a librarian for almost half a century, was a gold star mother from the First World War. But eventually everybody died.

"She invented the concep' 'ole folks home'," Dorothy told me, chuckling. "All her family dead. Husban' die thirty years ago. Even her chilun gone years ago. She out live 'em all, ev'y one of 'em."

After that speech I started thinking about longevity. What could be said about it? Is it an aspiration to live a hundred years? You live a hundred years and you're lucky? Nagh, that wasn't it. You live a hundred years and you're old, really old, too old. That's all there was to it. I quit touchin' her.

sweetie pie

Sweetie Pie was another one you couldn't touch. She was ninety years old and all day long she walked around and around the floor, keeping her joints limber, greeting everyone she passed with a nod or a "Howdy do." She must have walked five miles a day, that old gal.

Her feet were bad, a real tender foot she was, but that never discouraged her, just slowed her down I guess. She was a scrawny lizard of a woman, no teeth, raisiny caramel skin, parched hair. She wore a nightrobe and slippers everyday, all day long.

"She a ole ho', Richud," Dorothy told me. "Ole Mrs. Finnissey downstairs remember her from Clarksdale fi'ty years ago. Played piana and went with the mens at the ho'house. Moved up here when they close the place down. She likes da mens," Dorothy chuckled.

Sweetie Pie was witty, and she always had a nice word or a smile for everyone she passed, unless of course you challenged her like Kelvin:

"Hey Sweetie Pie, how's yo' sugarbowl?"

"Too sweet fo' yo' spoon."

"Ahh, you couldn't handle what I got."

"Da smalles' always talk the bigges'."

"How much you chargin'?"

"Mo'n you got."

Even Kelvin was no match for her. She won every verbal contest, hands down. No one ever got the better of her.

But her worst side came out when you touched her. I remember the first and only time I came in physical contact with her:

"Hey cutie," she stopped to flirt.

"S'up?" I replied.

"Need a date?"

"Sure do," and I started walking along with her. After two steps I made the fatal mistake of putting my arm around her shoulder.

"YOU GET YO' FUCKIN' HAN'S OFF ME, BOY! GOD-DAMN IT! GET THE FUCK AWAY FROM ME! SON OF A BITCH! YO' MOMMA SUCKED DICKS! GODDAMN YOU TO HELL, COCKSUCKAH! COCKSUCKAH!"

Oh man, she'd really come undone that ole gal if you touched her. Even that wizened old prune of a face would actually turn a faded shade of purple. She'd stand there letting you have it until you walked away. The funny thing was, her being senile, all you had to do was go around the corner and come back two seconds later and she'd greet you with that nod or that "Howdy do"—she'd have forgotten all about it.

She'd stop and lean against the wall and take a break every once in a while. Often was the time that I'd happen along and Dorothy'd be there chatting with her just like they were two ladies meeting on the street in Mississippi. Those two women could sure talk about nothing like it was something:

"How's them slippahs holdin' out? You sure puttin' the mileage on 'em, girl."

"They fine, fine. They lumpin' up in the midgel; all crooked now. Get me a eyeron and straighten 'em out sho' 'nough."

"That smart. How many laps you do so far?"

"I ain' countin' laps. I jus' walks. Flo sho' dirty t'day. Ain' no jainato's 'roun'. I show 'em where to sweep. Get they asses in gear."

Etc.

Sweetie Pie was incontinent. You'd come walking by her and as you got abreast of her—wham—you'd get a snoutful of her. Dorothy had the expression for this: "OOOOWEEE, YOU STANKY!"

There was always a scene when this happened:

"Don' touch me, I whup ya!" Sweetie Pie'd growl.

"You stanky. You got a load in yo' pan's, girl!"

"That my business," Sweetie Pie'd come back.

"It sho' is. But yo' walkin' these halls and makin' ev'ybody sick. Richud, cain you smell it over there?"

"Sure can."

"You leave me 'lone."

Then Dorothy, the sly old fox, would change the subject on her, shuffle the deck so to speak.

"Sing that ole tone fo' Richud," she'd say.

"What tone that?"

"You know what tone." She only knew one song. "Le's hear it."

Then Sweetie Pie'd settle her back against the wall and sing—

> "If the river was whiskey,
>   and the sea was cherry wine,
>   me and my bay ba,
>   stay drunk alllll . . . day long."

The way she bent those notes, man, you could just about hear her playing that piana sixty years ago, the tabacca smoke swirlin' around the ceiling fan, the loud voices making merry, the sweet negro sweat all pervasive. . . . But that last line never did rhyme. Then Dorothy would move in for the kill:

"Speakin' a water. It yo' baf day, girl."

"'Sat right?"

"Got a nice shampoo fo' yo' hair. Make it sof' an' sweet. Got razahs case you wanna shave them legs a yo's."

"Where chu get all dat?"

"Store."

"'Sat right?"

"Now do the sof' shoe. Richud watchin' you, he wanna see it."

She'd look over at me flirtatiously. "He a nice lookin' one."

"Ain'ee though," Dorothy would encourage. "Do the dance fo' 'im."

And Sweetie Pie'd shuffle those feet of hers and bend and straighten those knees in a flurry of rhythm.

"You still got it, girl," Dorothy would whistle.

"Never los' it."

And down the hall to the bath they'd go, talkin', just talkin' . . . "How them slippahs feelin'?"

"They all lump up in the midgel un'erneath. Gets me a eye-ron and straighten 'em back out, sho' 'nough."

Etc.

They set her up, those fiends, about a month after I had left the floor. Dorothy told me the story. Had one of the new "planted" aides try to physically change her chucks. Sweetie Pie, of course, smacked the girl upside the head. That was all they needed to transfer her over to the County.

She had spunk that ole gal. So long as she had a place to walk, she'd be all right. I don't worry about a person like Sweetie Pie, she's the rare type who can take care of herself anywhere, anytime—ninety years or nineteen years . . .

"If da worl' was made fo' Sweetie,
 Den da earth be one big park;
 Ev'y boy and girl and bay bay,
 Be jus' as happy assss . . . a clam."

'moke! 'moke! give me a puff!

Cap'n John was an old fireman without legs. He was chronically distracted. He sat in his wheelchair all day long, drumming his hands and tapping his fingers, and if he had any feet I'm sure they'd have been doing the same. He was a gnarly old buzzard, looked like a salty dog sailor, with a thick beard that dulled razors on contact. He liked to eat, and the only talking he did was to demand cigarettes, which were forbidden to him. "'Moke! 'Moke! Give me a puff!" he'd repeat all day long, unconsciously. Whenever Paul was off the floor, Dorothy would sneak him a couple of puffs, and that would make his day.

I adduced his constant fidgeting to his former profession—perhaps deep down inside a fireman is forever waiting for that siren announcing the conflagration to end all conflagrations. And because of his incorrigible distraction, he had no presence of mind.

His sister Irene came everyday at 2:15. The fact that Irene still retained her Irish brogue after decades away from her homeland was perhaps a sign of her undividable animus. She came after lunch and sat for an hour and a half with her brother "Johnny." Irene was married, had seven children, and was in her late fifties, so it wasn't like she was an old maid with nothing else to do. Usually she played cards with him, though Cap'n John was so distracted he couldn't get through a simple game of gin without throwing his cards down and calling for a "'Moke!"

"Johnny deary, you can't be smokin'. T'isn't good fer year health. Pick up year cards now and finish the ghim."

Irene was so sweet and gentle. Like Merry Mary, everyone was "deary" or "sweetie" or "honey" e.g., "Dorothy, honey, how are ye today?"

Dorothy and she were the perfect match. They'd get to talkin', Dorothy in her dialect, Irene in hers, and yet they'd get every word—nary a "Hunh?" or a "What's that you be saying, dear?" or a "Beggin' your pardon?"

For example:

"Tell me Dorothy, how's me Johnny been?"

"I tell ya poin' blank, Irene, he don' wanna get hisself up in da mo'nin' mos' times now. We gots ta fight wid him, he make such a fuss. 'Bout the only way to get him to behave hisself is if I dangles a cigarette fron' o' his nose."

"Is that a fact you say? I can't figure his insistence on the ceegarettes. T'wasn't his deely habit to be such a smoker as he seems. Never saw him put a ceegarette in his mouth in me life. His muder heeted the smoking, t'wouldn't let a body in her home with a lighted match, let 'lone a tabacco roll." Etc.

Some days Irene would sew for Cap'n John, or anyone else for that matter. If Dorothy knew of a shirt without the proper number of buttons, she'd bring it over to her and Irene would thank her for it. She'd sit there sewing and talking to her brother—just a comforting, soothing sight and sound she was. And thankless Cap'n John never acknowledged a word she said, never inquired about her life, her children, or his other brothers or sisters, nothing, just sat there tapping his fingers on the T.V. tray, crowing, "'Moke! 'Moke! Give me a puff!" And yet everyday there his sister sat, from 2:15 to 3:45, sewing and cooing like a dove.

Then Cap'n John took a turn for the worse.

Because Cap'n John's room was next to Shirley and Mon Cheri's room, Dorothy most days would help me get him up.

"OOOWEE, looky there! He messed hisself. Cap'n John, you soil yo' bed."

"'Moke! 'Moke! Give me a puff!"

"Richud, he startin' to go," she whispered to me behind her hand.

When Irene found out she was mortified. But the amazing thing was that she began showing up in the morning so that Dorothy, Kelvin, and I wouldn't have to clean up his messes. She insisted that it was her responsibility and not ours:

"I won't have you folks a cleanin' me brother's stool. T'ain't right for you to be tendin' to the likes of him. You have the others who're far worse off than Johnny needin' attention. I'll do it meself, and I'll be pleased for it, too—give me a reason to git up early."

Of course we had to get the administration involved to put a stop to it because she was serious—she was there five mornings in a row that first week.

Cap'n John's kidneys failed. They put him on renal dialysis, but he didn't last long. The day he passed away Irene came to give us all a token of her appreciation—CASH! A hundred-dollar bill for each of us. That made Kelvin's week.

"Here's just a little something from Johnny. 'Tisn't much. I'm embarrassed 'tisn't more. But Johnny appreciated all you good people done fer him. The service 'twill be tomorrow, given by the Bishop. He's our second cousin you know—Bishop O'Hagan. The family would be greatly honored if you folks came to the funeral service. The directions are there with yer cards." She had a handerchief and was constantly dabbing at her leaking eyes.

"Yo' brothah was a lucky mayn to have such a lovin' sister like you Irene," Dorothy solaced her. "He sho 'preciated all you done fo' him," she continued, stretching the truth a bit.

"I did what I could fer me poor brother. The Lord 'twasn't easy on Johnny. Took his legs from him. Never gave 'im a wife or family . . ." Then she began to sob, grimacing horrifically. Dorothy hugged her. She continued, "Bless his soul. He was always a lonely person, poor Johnny. He didn't ask much from life, just his daily bread."

"Well he ain' lonely no mo'. The Lawd wif him now," Dorothy patted her shoulder.

"Yes, and better company he is, to be sure, than his sister," Irene dabbed at her tear-filled peepers. "Poor Johnny, I never could figure what it 'twas he was waitin' for in life."

At the Irish wake, the man next to me standing at the open casket took out a pack of Winstons and put it in Cap'n John's breast pocket muttering, "You always was a cigarette moocher."

merry mary

Merry Mary was as pure and white as the newly fallen snow. To her, the world was good and right and just.

Almost from day one she waited for me outside on the front patio, under the rainbow. Rain, sleet, minus twenty degrees, she was there every morning at 7:00 A.M. to greet me. When I turned the corner she would come running, and by the time I made the steps leading up to the building, she would have me locked in her embrace. The people driving by on the street must have assumed that Merry Mary was my mother and that I, the son, had just returned home from a war. That embrace would remain until I pried her arms loose somewhere between the front entrance and the stairway door leading up to the third floor. When I played chess, for example, with one of the clients up on the fourth floor, Merry Mary would sit in the chair next to me, her arms locked onto one of my arms, asleep. She snored.

"She thank she yo' girlfrien' an' yo' mother bof," Dorothy explained to me when it first started to happen.

Merry Mary was a little butterball of a woman, five feet tall, fifty years old or so with snow white hair, gray-blue eyes, and a goatee and sideburns. She wore support hose, black shoes, and drab dresses. Her voice was elfish, and her speaking style childlike, with short, simple sentences that contained no idioms, no contractions. For example:

"I love you, Richard dear. You are so nice. Would you like to play cards with me today?"

There is something so profoundly confounding about goodness. Fellini tried to explain it in *La Strada* with Gelsomina and left us all crying. Wickedness, in contrast, is so common and predictable. There are just so many ways to kill and fuck (both literally and figuratively) your fellow man. In fact, the nuthouse was chock full of wickedness's victims. But goodness . . . the world cannot assimilate it.

I took Merry Mary's pureness personally because she had zeroed right in on me with her clinging arms and her sweet delight with the world around her, twisted as it was. I think my Catholic training subconsciously kicked in making me feel forever guilty and blasphemous and wicked around her. I understood how Zampano felt. In fact, around her I became Zampano—a crude, hedonistic brute with little or no tolerance for anything delicate. After a time, however, I began to try to understand my sense of discomfort around Merry Mary, so I examined her file like a monk. I was also able to glean enough information from Dorothy and the other aides to compile a picture of Merry Mary's life. It went something like this:

Merry Mary was an orphan and raised by nuns until the age of ten. At ten, she was adopted, or employed is a better way of putting it, by a well-to-do Scottish widow who lived in a huge mansion alone with Merry Mary and a few servants. This woman was a miser in the true sense of the word, and Merry Mary was taught that frugality, not cleanliness, was next to godliness. Fortunately, the woman died when Merry Mary was not yet eighteen, and only a token amount of money was given to her in the will. Merry Mary then moved back in with the nuns with the thought that she would become one of them. But she fell ill, very ill. For a year she lay in bed close to death, lapsing in and out of consciousness. Her recovery was slow, lasting another year more. The illness seemed to have affected her mind, and at twenty years of age she was dismissed from the nunnery as unfit to do God's work and employed in another wealthy household as a nanny. Her charge was a three-year-old girl named Alicia. She loved that child with all of her heart and soul. They travelled to Europe together, and out West, and to Florida and the Caribbean. But the child died within a few years. Merry Mary never recovered. What little capacity she had for work was lost. The sisters took her back, but soon after committed her to the huge County mental hospital. Once there she was found to be harmless, and for the next twenty-five years she was passed from nursing home to nursing home until she ended up at the Rainbow.

Merry Mary was the heart and soul of the Rainbow. She lived on the first floor in the first room as you walked in. Any news, any birthdays, any event Merry Mary not only knew about it, but she had probably organized or discovered it. She distributed Holy Communion to the Catholics on Sunday during the mass up on the fourth floor; called the numbers at the weekly Bingo games; walked around daily with handmade birthday cards for everyone to sign; she even wrote, typed, and xeroxed a monthly newsletter entitled, "The Rainbow News." Occasionally I would contribute a movie review or a restaurant review or an editorial. Merry Mary was everything and everywhere.

When we played cards she would talk about how wonderful and dear Dorothy was or Gloria was or Ronald Reagan was or John Wilkes Booth. It didn't matter who they were, they were "wonderful" and "dear." But I was the most wonderful and dear. There was no one more wonderful and dear than Richard as far as Merry Mary was concerned. That was because I was the only one contrite enough to pay any attention to her. Everyone in that place avoided her like the plague. Occasionally, the administration would throw her a bone, but that's because they were using her in their ploy to clean house.

Every day Merry Mary smote me with her embraces and acco-
lades and goodness, and every day I turned my cheek and let
her deal me another blow.

Then a thought hit me like a ton of bricks. I was playing
chess with a private client and Merry Mary was stuck to my
arm snoring. An alarm went off in my head: "What's going to
happen when I leave this job?"

Like Zampano, I had to ditch Merry Mary somehow and it
wasn't going to be easy. I began by sneaking in the back way in
the morning in order to avoid her. She would always come up
to the third floor and find me and sulk and pout about how I
didn't play cards with her anymore, or greet her in the morning or sign her birthday cards or write articles for the
newsletter.

And like Zampano, the guilt began to overwhelm me. I
started having nightmares. In these dreams I was a murderer, a
maniac, a monster, and the world was trying unsuccessfully to
keep me from killing its babies and grandmothers and kittens.
This was all Merry Mary's doing.

Obviously the avoidance tactic was a rotten idea. I went
back to the old routine of greeting Merry Mary in the morning, playing cards with her, letting her sleep on my arm while I
played chess, writing stupid movie reviews for the newsletter,
and signing her goddamn birthday cards. The nightmares
stopped. And that's the way it went until the day I left there.

If there is no place in society for goodness, where does it belong, pray tell? We certainly idolize it and pray to it and even
aspire to it, yet we can't live with it. Perhaps goodness is like a
mirror of truth, and when we are around it we see ourselves as
we truly are. If that's the case, then the Merry Marys of the
world are doomed to martyrdom and pariahdom.

grand mal seizure

It's not every day that a man melts in this world. But when a grand mal seizure strikes, anything is possible, I guess . . .

Milton was a tall man, a big man, six feet four, fifty-five to sixty years old, no crazier but no less crazy than the rest. He shuffled about as most of them did with ill-fitting shoes and snot in his nose. His hair, what was left of it, was bone gray, cut short to the stems on the sides of his head. He had a big round nose, fat, swollen cheeks, and ruby red lips as if he were a trumpet player or something. Milton was epileptic, and as such was denied full access to the work world during his youth. His file listed his trade as baker, but the periods of time that he actually plied his craft were few and far between. Over the years too many grand mal seizures caught up to him and led to his institutionalization. His every move was gangly and sloppy. His outstanding characteristic was his blubbering. He blubbered every minute of the day, rarely uttering a recognizable word.

But even more distinctive about Milton was Eulalia. They were a couple, not legally or even admittedly as far as Milton was concerned, but they were an item. It was Eulalia's doing. She was a manipulator type like many psychotics. Eulalia was a marvel in her own right. She had long, white-gray hair that she brushed straight back. I can't say it was becoming, but it certainly made her look archetypically witch-like. She was ugly, that's for sure, with a storybook, aquiline nose that she peered down so smugly. She was Milton's age, or thereabouts. Listed as a paranoid schizophrenic, she'd been in and out of institutions most of her life, though as a woman in her twenties she had worked for a short period of time as a French teacher in a private school for girls. In her file it explains that she had been fired from the school because of an "inappropriate affair with one of the employees." This last word always fired my imagination, and I had convinced myself that she had been caught screwing the janitor—a vocation that she latently aspired to, and only when she was committed was it allowed to fully manifest itself.

She spent her waking hours dressed in a nightrobe, cleaning and straightening and neatening everything in sight. Most of the time she'd have a broom in hand and she'd sweep and sweep and sweep. Mount Shirley hated her guts and at least once a day would verbally assault her. "You're fuckin' insane! Look at you! You're the worst one here! You're so pitiful! Playing the great lady. Look at how ugly you are." That was Paul's cue to come by and give Mount Shirley a pill. Shirley didn't like Eulalia because Eulalia smiled all the time; she wasn't down in the dumps like Shirley and the others. She wore a constant smile, a self-satisfied smirk, an arrogant grin that advertised her belief and understanding of the true ordered nature of things. Perhaps she was Lucretius reincarnated. Conversely, Milton was a slob, a floppy, gangly, blubbering, slobbering slob. Oh, and she tittered too. She tittered the way that Milton blubbered, only her tittering made sense. It was a straightener's language, a singsong titter-while-you-work tittering—"This goes here . . . that there . . . oh my they make such a mess . . ." Etc. Whereas Milton's blubbering was just plain gobbledygook—"Blabboof, blaaebel, blaelglbla . . ." Etc.

They were a perfect match, and that's why she loved him so, worshipped his every sneeze and slobber and blubber. He'd sit in a chair and blubber and she'd take the chair next to him and hold his hand and reassure him that she'd straighten it all out, he didn't have to worry. I had nothing against either one of them. As a matter of fact, they were pretty high scorers—good at washing and toileting and dressing and feeding. They were an okay pair. But then Milton melted . . .

When I recall that man, the way he turned out, no smile, no snicker comes to my lips. Rather, I get a kind of sickening feeling in the pit of my stomach. Like Kelvin said, "Ain' nothin' funny there."

She was in the chair next to him, as usual, with that boastful smile of hers, a smile that said, "Yes, I'll straighten it all out, you slobs, you disorganized fools." Then, as I walked by them, the ever-slouching and blubbering Milton suddenly went pouring out of that high-backed chair and onto the floor like a quart of milk. I was with Bob White and I quickly parked him in a nearby chair and went to help Milton get back up into his seat. Now I remember, even at that moment, looking down on that puddle of a man on the floor and saying to myself, "Something's terribly wrong here," because he was blubbering doubly fast and he was lying there like a pool of urine. Eulalia, too, sensed something was askew and was shaking her head pensively and probably telling herself that she would change his shirt and pants once he stood up. But Milton would never stand again.

Milton was a big man, a gangly man, and when I went to help him to his feet I could've just as well been trying to prop up an overcooked noodle. I yanked on one part of him and the other side leaked out. I gathered the two ends together and the middle sagged away. I recall stopping and assessing the situation, scratching my head and shaking it at the fidgeting and tittering Eulalia. She reflected my bemused expression. Then I tried coaxing him to his feet: "Milton, get up now," I said with authority. No way!

"Blabbofblaaebelblaelglba . . ." he foamed, his cheeks and lips all red and beginning to pile high with froth while the blubbering came out in one continuous stream. There was no question in my mind, it was a reenactment of the Dumpty Debacle, and there was no putting him back together.

I called for help and Paul and Kelvin joined me. The three of us put him in the chair, but he just ran right down and onto the floor before we could catch him. We tried several times with the same results. Paul finally got a couple of posies, and we tied him tightly to that chair as if he were a seat cover. And there he stuck, like a jellied scarecrow, dripping down to the floor pathetically from his perch. What a sight he was as we stood looking at him while Eulalia, poor Eulalia, busied herself around the area sweeping, straightening, and occasionally wiping his mouth with a kleenex.

"That mayn ain' right," Kelvin echoed my thoughts exactly.

"Grand mal seizure," Paul shook his head in response, as if that were enough to explain it.

"Yeah, but ain' they 'spose to shake 'n bake if they be havin' one a those?" Kelvin queried.

"Usually." Paul himself didn't know.

If the word "melted" had come to mind right then, I would have shouted it out.

But that word came later. Milton couldn't be contained. They put him in his bed and he leaked out and onto the floor. They tied him in the chair and he sagged horrifically. They tried tying him up in the bed, but he'd leak over the sides and we'd find him dripping pitifully towards the floor. And poor Eulalia, like an animal she was, like an animal acts when its mate has been stricken mortally—tittering about him, cleaning and straightening and sweeping in double time, checking and rechecking her mate.

It's true Big Bird wanted them all gone, but this was different, this was a matter of professional pride. You can't call someone to take a client away just because he's had an epileptic fit. Alcatraz didn't call Sing Sing just because one of its prisoners stuck a penknife in another. Yet, this was something completely different. A man had melted and there was no one to be called in who could solidify him. Not that they didn't try. People came from all over, state officials, psychologists, ichthyologists, gelatinologists, eminent specialists in every related field. They all came to have a go at liquified Milton who had become quite the attraction in his own room with the padding on the floor and the wastebasket piled high with kleenex. But no matter how hard they tried, they couldn't solidify Milton again.

Finally one day they just came and took him away. He was the first to go, ironically. I have no idea where they took him, perhaps to an aquarium. I just remember Eulalia that day as they laboriously carted him off. She was tittering no longer. She had become a bereaving spouse with that smug smile of hers wiped clean. But in her eyes I could see that she had an answer. She knew that she was the only one who could help Milton, could at least keep him contained. Perhaps this is what made her so quiet. She suddenly looked up at me as the door closed behind Milton and his escorts and said, "They'll never keep him together, he's . . . he's . . ." and for some reason she couldn't articulate the word that had been on the tip of my tongue from the onset of this calamity.

"Melted!" I exhaled with a hearty gust, hearing it and thinking it for the very first time.

She nodded her head sadly in agreement. She stood there a moment looking up at me still nodding her head, thinking that perhaps it might have been nicer that way, even nicer than it had been before he'd melted—she could have been there, always busy, sweeping, straightening, containing him when he'd spread out too much. Yes, that's what her nodding was all about, but he was gone now and no one but she and I knew what was best for poor old Milton. Poor old Milton . . .

I hope I never in my life have to see another person melt. Terra firma . . . corpus firma . . . that's the stuff for me.

baldy

After Milton had melted, I ran to Nick the next day for solace and guidance. I was frazzled, "upaside down" myself.

"Okay my young buddy. Nobody in dee shop today, Nick gotta lots time take'a care you."

"Give me the works, Nick." I plopped myself down dejectedly in the chair and stared at my scruffy mug in the mirror for a couple of seconds, uncomprehendingly. "I don't know Nick," I started right in, needing to get it off my chest. "That goddamn place! That job! Those people! It's startin' to get to me. I mean, I'm trying and all, I am, but I . . . I . . . Christ, I'm losing my friggin' hair it's got me so stressed out. I'm gonna go bald if I continue to work there, I tell ya."

"What'a you sayin', my buddy?"

"I'm talkin' about the job! No, I'm talkin' about my hair," skirting the issue. "All this crazy goddamn work's making me lose it, I swear. I'm finding all sorts of strands and clumps in my brush these days. I think I'm going bald, Nick!" I ran my tremulous fingers through my wayward bristles.

"Ha ha, no no! Don'a you worry, ev'ybody lose'a hair, ev'ry day. T'ousands hairs lost ev'ry day, ev'rybody. You no'a need worry 'bout that, my buddy. You gotta good hair, t'ick'a hair, you no'a need worry," he reassured me so confidently.

"But my grandfather was bald," I offered accusingly.

Head bent, he went over to the hot lather machine and filled his palm with foam, then walked back up behind me and began to lather my face with the hot cream. There was a heavy silence. "You gran'father baldy? Who gran'father?" he asked with concern.

"My mother's father," I replied.

His concerned look deepened. And that was the last thing I saw as he lowered me down and pressed a hot towel in a pile over my already lathered face. "Hmmm, you mother father baldy, you may be baldy," he said apologetically, still pressing on the towel. "Now, you father father baldy, you no baldy," conciliatorily. "You father baldy, you no baldy," reassuringly. "You father father no baldy, you father baldy, you may be baldy. You mother father no baldy, you mother brother baldy, you baldy. You father no baldy, you father brother baldy, you father mother father baldy, you baldy," singing out in rhythm. "You father no baldy, you mother father father baldy, you may be baldy. You father mother father—"

"Nick! Nick!" I had to interject.

"What's that buddy?" pulling the towel off.

"What if your mother's bald?"

"You mother baldy? Ha ha, then you baldy baldy!"

After the genetics lesson, I wasn't quite so agitated. But later on in the session, about the time he was trimming around my ears, we got back to the troubling subject. Actually, he brought it up first.

"Nick proud'a you workin' over there, no'a complains, college graduate workin'a wit' dee poor people like dat, learnin' 'bout people. You especial person, buddy."

"Yeah, special all right."

There was a long silence during which time he was contemplating the various implications of my cynical response. Then he commenced with the pep talk. "Nobody in dee whole worl' doin'a what you doin', workin'a over dere. Nobody. Ev'rybody out makin'a money, t'inkin' 'bout buyin' car, house, boat, findin'a nice wife, gettin'a married. But you, you learnin' 'bout life, 'bout peoples, seein'a what life really like, goin'a write you book. *Che bravo.*"

"Yeah," I croaked meekly. There was silence for a moment. He clipped and I listened. The snapping steel scissors filled my head completely.

"They changin' that'a place, hunh, really cleanin' it up?" he asked, snapping me out of my daze.

"Well, you know what they're doing, don't ya?" My tone was rather strident and it must have surprised him because he stopped clipping and looked harshly at my image in the mirror.

"No, what'a you mean?"

"They're trying to get rid of everybody."

"What'a you sayin'? That make'a no sense."

"The new owner's trying to get rid of all the Medicaid patients; she's trying to turn the place into a private home, get private-paying clients so she can make more money. You didn't know that?"

"How'a he gonna do dat?"

"She. Simple, just send the ones there over to the county mental facility and bring in new private-paying clients. She's advertising in the *Sun-Times,* I've seen it."

"Never heard'a such t'ing like'a dat before." He seemed very surprised.

"That's what's going on. I thought you knew that."

"Know that? What'a Nick know? I jus'a come once mont' cut'a dee hair. I no see new peoples 'round dee place. Jus' dee first floor some'a new peoples."

"Yeah, that's where it's starting. That's their showpiece, the first floor. Like a weed, like a cancer, it's starting there and it's eventually going to grow right up through the roof. You watch. But we're seeing to it that the clients stay put," I boasted.

"You'a do what?"

"Dorothy, Kelvin, and I, we're making sure the staff doesn't have cause to send them over to the County."

"I still'a no un'erstand what'a you sayin', buddy."

"Look, in order for them to send the people over to the county, they have to have proof that these people are a danger to themselves and others. Since we're the ones who work with them all day, the aides, we're the ones who would report any cases of endangerment. But instead, we're guarding them. People like Floyd and Shirley, you know them?"

"Sure, sure, Floyd."

"Well, they should've been gone months ago. That's what were doing. We're making sure they stay put."

"Now'a I see." He was silent for a long time as he cut the hair. I finally had to carry on the conversation.

"That's why I'm all bent out of shape. It's not right, you know? You can't do that to people. You can't take a person's home away, especially people like that. You can't take advantage of helpless people."

"Hah!" he barked out in mocking laughter, the one blast echoing for a good while about the mirrored room.

"What are you laughing at?"

"At'a what'a you say. Helpless peoples dee first get dee advantage taken out of them. Dat's'a how it'a work from dee bottom to'a dee top. Most helpless peoples have'a dee least, least helpless have'a dee most. It never change." He shrugged his shoulders. "But ev'rybody just'a little helpless. Even'a you. You sittin' in'a my chair, I give'a you haircut an'a shave. I could'a say dee bill twenty-five dollar an'a you pay me, even if'a I lie, even if'a it only fifteen dollar."

"But you won't."

"Maybe not, you'a my friend, but if you not'a my friend, I gonna get jus'a little bit, take'a 'vantage jus'a little bit, see how'a much I can'a get. Dat's'a business. Dat's'a life."

"Geez, I thought you'd be upset about this."

"'Bout what?"

"Never mind."

When I went to go, he wouldn't take my money. He clasped me on the neck and squeezed tight with his muscular hand. What a grip! We stood face to face, his shiny pate glowing under my nose. "You especial person, buddy; you keep'a doin' what you do. Nick'a proud you. An'a don'a you worry 'bout changin' t'ings an'a make'a dee worl' better place, that's not'a you job. You job changin'a youself, makin'a youself better, that dee only way make'a dee worl' better."

"Yeah," I squeaked.

bob white

Down's syndrome is a limbo. And Bob White existed in this way station between Heaven and Hell, consciousness and unconsciousness, humanity and bestiality. Though surrounded by the schizophrenic, the psychotic, the syphilitic, the demented, the Down's syndrome was the most foreign realm for me. In the others I could at least feel inside that at one time in their history they walked upon a common ground, but in the Down's syndrome this mutual zone never existed. It's futile to try to understand them. I remember I even attempted to compare— "All right then, let's say that Bob White has the intelligence of the average chimpanzee . . ." But that didn't work because a chimpanzee is sound and whole unto himself, he has arrived at his destination in the evolutionary journey. Bob White was nowhere, neither consumed in a world of delusion or monomania, nor degenerating hopelessly toward doom. He was nowhere, not even cloud nine.

Bob White was the oldest Down's syndrome I had ever seen, and now, in retrospect, I realize this was his bane because in today's world modern developmentalists are able to help a Down's syndrome live a far more human existence. Unfortunately, he had spent his entire life in the institution which meant that his defective faculties were allowed to lie fallow during the most crucial periods of their conditioning, and later when attempts were made to teach an old dog new tricks, so to speak, the little tractability that once existed had long since petrified.

Bob White was a little quail of a man, no more than five feet in height, with straight, bodiless gray hair which looked best combed back. I estimated his age at about fifty only because he was once visited by a brother, a very normal looking man in his mid fifties. There were no other relations. His overall complexion was sallow, and inside his pants he had a herniated scrotum which was swollen to the size of a grapefruit. It had been that way for decades; never been fixed. Such is the cruelty of a system that actually does put a price tag on human life. He floated through the day like a somnambulist, his deeply set eyes neither focused or glazed. I'd wake him in the morning and he'd pop his head up out of the sheets as if he'd inadvertently dozed off while waiting for the water to boil. He'd climb out of bed fully awake without the slightest sign of recent slumber save for the gobs of sand gathered like maggot infestation at the corners of his eyes. I always wondered why this was, why his body would process so much sand, but I never found that out.

He spoke as if he meant to say something to me, but the words, the grammar or the lack thereof, was nonsensical—no verbs, mostly nouns with articles. And the voice was a nasalized drone, strange in resonance, perhaps caused by an incomplete sinus canal, or an underdeveloped voice box, or both. "Toothbrush . . . shirt . . . the shoes . . . my shirt . . . ha ha ha ha . . . " He laughed, or made a sound like a laugh. But it wasn't a laugh, it was a primordial sound, a sound that is programmed into all humankind, only in the Down's syndrome it doesn't ring true—like a bell that's struck while a hand rests on its flange, or a muted horn when blown.

He was agonizingly slow. Slow because he had no purpose, no routine. Without a routine he was unaware of the imminent meal, the need to dress, to eat, to seek entertainment. He was bereft of all these instincts. Everything had to be learned anew each day, each hour, each minute. And I just didn't have the time. Who did?

My routine, contrary to his, was very rigid. I had exactly forty-five minutes to wake up, dress, and deliver a dozen male malfunctions to the table before the breakfast cart arrived. Bob White was, like Fred for Kelvin, the big wall in this obstacle course I called a job. Try dressing a human being who has never been dressed before, who doesn't know what a belt is, which shoe goes on which foot, how to put on a pair of pants. There was only one thing he could do, for some reason, he could put on any one of his flannel shirts and button it.

He didn't like to be rushed. The more you rushed him the more confused he became. So he'd resist you. This was trying to say the least. Plus, he pissed his pants every night so he'd have to be changed each morning. After yanking and swatting his hand and tugging and scolding and pulling, I'd have him dressed. Every moment of it was a struggle. Then I'd lead him by the hand down the hall to a high-backed chair, take a posey and tie him securely to it. Why would I tie him to his chair? Simple:

On my first encounter with Bob White, I was alone and knew nothing about him. I got him up, put on his underwear, and began to dress him, though he seemed determined to do it his own way and in his own time. I assumed too much. I laid out his wardrobe in a row on his bed, helped him get into his flannel shirt, saw that he could button it himself and was convinced he could handle the rest, so off I went to my next charge. At breakfast a half-hour or so later, Dorothy's nose for imperfection was sniffing the air.

"Where Bob White at?"

"Isn't he here?" I asked in surprise.

"You leave him 'lone, Richud?" Dorothy asked suspiciously.

"Yeah, I left him in his room to finish dressing."

"You didn'!" she guffawed. "He cain' dress hisself, chile,"

she shook her head and began to march down the hall. I joined her. We quickly arrived at his room. "Would you looky here. OOOWEE he confuse'!"

Bob White was in the middle of the room, a half-dozen pairs of pants strewn all over the bed, every drawer was pulled open, every hanger was pulled out of form and lay on the closet floor in a pile, and he was in the process of putting on the last of his half-dozen flannel shirts. He looked like a flannel-clad astronaut.

"You cain' leave him 'lone by hisself, Richud," Dorothy admonished with a comforting smile. Then we straightened up the mess.

The next time that I assumed with Bob White wasn't quite as innocuous. About a week later, I did everything for him as instructed—changed his underwear, put on his shirt, pants, shoes and socks, brushed his hair, tightened his belt, even helped him blow his nose before I led him down to the breakfast table. As I was leading him to his seat, Kelvin called out to me from a nearby room requesting immediate assistance. Not but eight feet from his usual chair, I pushed him gently toward it, pointing to it, then I slipped quietly away to help Kelvin clean Bobby's behind. Twenty minutes later the police were alerted—MISSING PERSON.

Bob White had, apparently, veered slightly left of the chair, gone down the side stairway to the basement and then out the open delivery door into the frigid February morning. Clad only in a pair of khaki pants, a flannel shirt, brown leather loafers, a T-shirt and a brush in his shirt pocket, he wandered the East Side without a clue. Two hours later they found him in a women's clothing shop with half a dozen blouses wrapped around his stunted frame. The image I hold of that scene, though I wasn't actually there when they retrieved him, was of a dark-haired, well-fashioned, woefully aging woman holding a phone to her ear, hand over her mouth, peeking at him from behind a row of coats, describing his every move to the 911 dispatch operator in a whisper—"He's putting on another blouse. Yes . . . Now he's taking the hanger and twisting it . . ."

Later on my impatience toward Bob White evolved into appreciation. I found out that he responded tenderly to affection, and, in fact, seemed to thrive on it. We had many a fine bath together even though he was skittish about water.

He was discarded during the great purge months later, sent over to the County with all the rest.

The Down's syndrome, no doubt, has been around since the beginning. I believe the Down's syndrome person has lived just as he or she lives today—under the auspices of human decency. Perhaps the Down's syndrome represents a covenant between God and man as atonement for original sin. Or perhaps the Down's syndrome is God himself, conducting an undercover operation to test our righteousness. Any way you look at it, there's a lot of God to be found in the Down's syndrome.

the blackhead

There are moments in life when we see the bottom. The very bottom of experience is as solid and impassable as a concrete cellar floor. We rove through life, our cognizance humming from the mundane, when out of the blue we come face to face with the endall. Soldiers in war are greeted by it when next to them their buddy's head is splattered by a well-aimed bullet. Policemen meet up with it on the interstates when they observe, under the twisted piles of steel, lying on the vinyl seats of small cars, scattered body parts. Doctors, obdurate and well-prepared as they are to experience the end, occasionally run into it when, opening a body, they find the fetid oozing offal of a malignant tumor. And yes, the nurse's aide has his encounter.

It was the normal kind of a day at the nuthouse. Lunch was over, the clients were content. Pills were in effect. Curly needed his bath, and both Kelvin and I were leading him to the tub. We worked well together, Kelvin and I, and on occasion we would spend the entire day working in tandem. This was a tacit agreement and just happened naturally. Not every day, but sometimes.

I named him Curly. Curly was a dead ringer for the Three Stooges' Curly, and so that's what I called him—inspired by co-incidental Fred. He went along with the name, Kelvin did, but

I don't think he ever watched the Stooges. I don't think the black folk go in for the Stooges.

Anyway, Curly couldn't talk, but he could squeak in a high pitched sound like a whining pup. He didn't make this sound very often, he needed prodding to get it out. He was a spooky character all right. He would skulk around the halls playing with his fingers. I never read his file nor took much interest in him, though I probably should have. Why is it that there are some people, daft or otherwise, who inspire us with no interest, who somehow remain invisible to the majority? I remember in high school seeing kids on graduation day walk up to receive their diplomas whom I had never seen before, yet they had gone to the same school as I for six years. All I remember is that no one came to visit Curly, and everybody pretty much ignored him, clients and staff alike.

Kelvin was talking about his get-rich-quick scheme, his favorite subject—

"You ain' 'spose' to do it fo' exacise, you does it fo' fun. A duo pogo stick. Think o' the name, Duo Pogo. It a concep', you know?"

"Get that dirt spot on his chest," I interrupted him as he washed Curly's back with a washcloth.

"That no dirt spot. That a blackhead."

"No way. That!" pointing, he nodding. "It's the size of a thumbtack. Jesus Fucking Christ!" I picked at it. It didn't budge.

"That a blackhead awright. Bigges' blackhead known to man. They don' get no bigger than that."

"That's really unbelievable!"

"Ain' never squeezed it. I usually squeeze them thangs when I sees 'em. But that too big, might do sompin' bad. We could get in trouble sompin' happen like it start bleedin' or get infected 'n shit. It so big the doctor need to operate to get it off," kidding, and then not really.

"Imagine what's underneath it," I thought aloud.

And all this while poor old Curly was looking at us suspiciously, his eyes darting back and forth between Kelvin and me.

Then Kelvin felt bold, his boldness spurned on by the prospect of money. "How much you give me if I squeeze it off?"

"Get outa town!"

"I serious."

At this point, and knowing Kelvin as well as I did, I had a hunch that this was all a scam of some sort that he had concocted to extract more money from me. Like I said, his great passion was to get rich quick, and I played a key role in stoking his fire of inspiration. I stared at the blackhead and looked over at Kelvin's big, anxious eyes. Scam or no scam, I couldn't see how it could be other than what it appeared. Truly a herculean proposition.

"If you squeeze that off we'll be square. You won't owe me, what is it now . . . thirty bucks?"

"Rich, cousin, looky that thang. I could get fired sompin' happen here."

Thirty bucks was a lot of money to me. He had borrowed it slowly, five dollars at a time. I expected to be repaid. But then reality set in—who was I kidding? The moment I gave him the money, that was the end of it. "Well how much you want?"

"Leas' another twenty, man."

"Five."

"Rich, cousin . . . "

"All right, ten then."

"Deal."

"Really, you're going to do it?" I couldn't believe it, $40 or no $40, it was an awesome event.

"Shake on it." We shook, Curly between us, his head underlined by our conspiring hands.

Kelvin found the washcloth he'd let fall beneath Curly's leg, and ran the hot water on it till it was steaming. Barely able to hold it, he dangled it from his finger tips and like a crane slowly lowered it into place. Curly began to whine, adding a mounting tension to the already tingly anticipation. Kelvin, face intent, his big black nostrils flared, pressed the steaming cloth on the "Little Nigger" as he referred to it. He held it there a good while before he removed the cloth and shot me a quick, "This is it" glance, and began to squeeze testingly. He pulled his fingers away to look. Nothing. Poor old Curly, he was looking down beyond his chin, his face all beaded with sweat, his cheeks flushed red with fear. Kelvin began to squeeze again, this time in earnest, gritting his teeth, his black fingers taut, the veins on his neck bulging. He gasped and stopped abruptly. Our heads moved in closer to examine it. Still nothing. But wait, there was a bent shape to it, as if it had been upset, and like a picture on the wall it was off center. He took the washcloth and again steamed it up under the vaporous tapwater and pressed it against that "Little Nigger." He threw the cloth in the tub with a plop and locked down on that blackhead as if ready to battle to the death. He squeezed and squeezed, grunting, gritting his teeth, as Curly whined and looked fearfully down at his chest. One second went by, two seconds, three seconds . . . Kelvin's eyes were wild, furious, his thumbs verging on white with pressure. Then suddenly the huge lid began to rise. If a crowd had been there watching, you would have heard great gasps and sighs. Slowly it rose at first, then in a long steady assent. Behind it followed a yellowish clear solid. Up, up it ascended, the color of the anti-ballistic changing from the original clear yellow, to white, then to gray. It was like some beast rising from an ancient tomb.

"Hooooolee shit!" I ejaculated under my breath.

An inch . . . two inches . . . three inches . . . four inches.

"HOOOOLEE SHIT!" I cawed.

Curly was whining at such a high pitch by this point that he must have been upsetting all the dogs in the neighborhood.

His face was red and drenched with sweat, and his eyes were in total confusion as if he didn't know whom to blame—Kelvin or himself or the blackhead.

"There you go," Kelvin held out his hand offering the pencil-sized pus for inspection. I glanced at it momentarily then fished my wallet out and extracted an Alexander. We made the exchange. Kelvin grabbed the bill with his free hand then tipped his palm and let the blackhead roll into mine. I took that blackhead and held it close to my eyes—THUD—my nose hit bottom.

floyd

Floyd had one testicle. Seeing a scrotum containing one lonely testicle is a shocking, awe-inspiring sight, especially for a male. From that moment on, I was a fervent Floyd fan.

Floyd had always been an imp. From day one, after placement in his first foster home at the age of six, he had been trouble spelled with a capital T. No home could keep him, no school could control him. Five foster homes, eight schools, and twelve years later, Floyd was finally discarded into the institution. Like most of the people there, his mania fermented like rare wine. But Floyd was different. His mania was compelling, attractive, suspenseful. It was simple really—Floyd was on a mission.

Floyd was also enemy number one for the administration. They wanted him out of there in the worst way. But again, this all had to be done in accordance with the law. They pined for proof of his disorderly conduct, and he knew it all too well.

Floyd wasn't dangerous, he was a scream. Floyd looked like a bug or a gnarled hirsute version of Inspector Clouseau. He was walleyed, about five feet two, with a long, severly pointed chin, thick whiskers, no neck, a big nose, and a voice like a cartoon character. It was raspy, not low and not high in tone, and it had a buzz to it like locusts whirring against a screen window.

You could never fully understand him. Perhaps he wanted it that way. He dressed absurdly. Since the state provided just $100 worth of clothing a year for these people, most had only a couple pairs of pants, shoes, socks, some shirts, and a jacket or two. Fittingly, Floyd wore a raincoat. The raincoat covered the only pair of pants he had and they would have fit a man twice his size. He wore sneakers, nice white, well-fitting sneakers, something which he was very proud of. He was lopsided too. If you stood behind him and watched him scuttle down the hall in his lickety-split gait, you'd laugh at the way his entire body was slanted to the left as if he were walking on the far edge of a well-crowned path.

Kelvin was into Floyd too, but his ulterior motives weren't the same as mine. I liked Floyd for who he was as a para-person and what he stood for; Kelvin just liked him for his chin.

"C'mere, Floyd," Kelvin growled.

"ZZun ZZuh," shaking his head no.

"Git yoself over here," pulling him into a nearby room.

"ZZZZeye ZZZno ZZZZno ZZZoo ZZZoo ZZZrr."

"What?" grabbing the chin and squeezing it. "You gettin' a shave today. You really crusty, you know that?"

"ZZZuh ZZZZuh," shaking his head, his walleyes flashing.

"Don' give me no shee, Floyd," squeezing his chin harder so that Floyd grimaced.

"ZZZeye, ZZZick ZZZah ZZZig ZZZeel ZZZack."

"Who cares, Floyd." Kelvin could understand him, but I couldn't. "Looky yo' pans'! Tuck yo' shirt in."

Floyd stood defiantly. Kelvin squeezed the chin viciously again and Floyd submitted to the request. Done, he stood insolently, waiting to be dismissed, arms at his sides like a prisoner.

" 'Member, you shavin' today, you hear? An' you better not try an' hide or I kick yo' fanny hard this time. Go on."

And he scurried away.

Unlike Inspector Clouseau who seemed always to create disaster inadvertently wherever he went, Floyd wreaked havoc surrepticiously and deliberately. Old ladies walking down the hall would be pushed over suddenly without provocation or any clue as to who had done it; clients' simple belongings like toothpaste and toothbrushes, pictures, alarm clocks, hair brushes, etc. would disappear; fire alarms would go off; chairs would spontaneously lose a leg; feces and urine would be found in the most unlikely places. This was all the work of one inspired man. Everyone knew it was Floyd, it was a given, yet nothing could be done.

Paul, the floor nurse, would get really pissed sometimes, especially if he found a big stinking turd in the bathtub. When this happened he'd make a foray into Floyd's room and find some incriminating evidence, like Bobby's missing toothbrush, and then he'd come back and posey Floyd to a chair for good measure. Floyd, of course, would take his punishment with defiance and triumph. Paul's face would turn the most brilliant shade of red. And best of all, Floyd, being the secret agent of his mind, would slip out of the posey like Houdini within an hour's time. Then Paul's face would turn incandescent red.

The administration wanted him out in the worst way, but thanks to us he stayed put, so in essence he represented our victory over them. But even more than that, he was entertainment, and he gave us all a sense of purpose and hope that all was not lost. With Floyd around, anything could happen at any moment. It was a great comfort to have this feeling. Paul was convinced that Floyd didn't take his pills, he only pretended. As I said, he was on a mission, and he was never at rest or comfortable or submissive.

Any of the normal dealings with him were difficult. Meals, he'd bring his plate back to his room. Baths were a struggle. He wouldn't let you soap him or shampoo his hair, and yet he wouldn't do any of it himself. He'd sit in the tub eyeing you hatefully like a prisoner his captor. Consequently, you had to forcefully administer care and he could be incredibly elusive even sitting there in the tub. Shaving was the only thing he'd submit to. But on days when he was to be shaved he was hard to find. Kelvin and I would have to drop everything and hunt him down. We'd separate, I'd start looking in the basement and Kelvin would start on the fourth floor and we'd meet in the middle somewhere. Sometimes we never did find him.

Floyd's days were numbered. Even with the aides on his side, we knew the administration would eventually catch up with him. Big Bird and Gloria had their spies amongst the ranks of clients. Not that these clients were aware of it, they were too stupid or too pure to understand this. Secretly they had been collecting and documenting eyewitness accounts of Floyd's malfeasance. They needed to log just one more egregious violation and the Sheriff's office would be summoned and off to the County he'd go.

Paul was downright witch-like on that fateful day. Wow! He had overmedicated Bobby so that the poor baby was frozen solid in his usual chair. We kept out of his way on days when he was like this. We all have our moods, but with Paul, the hateful fat boy, he became the devil incarnate.

Gloria, the head nurse, came on the floor just fuming because a prospective private's family was touring the building, and Floyd, our resident Fido, had piddled down the stairs and they had been forced to splash through it to get to their destination. Paul flew into an absolute rage. He summoned Kelvin and me and ordered us to hunt down "the little bastard." We found him on the top floor, in the game closet, eating a stolen batch of homemade cookies. With heavy hearts we escorted him back down to Paul who, with harmful intent, totally abused poor Floyd—taking him from us by the ear, he pulled him over to a high-backed chair and slammed him into the seat, his face verging on purple with anger. Next, he reviled him up and down while far too tightly tying him to the seat with a posey. "You're going to sit there, Mister, until you piss on yourself, that's how long it'll be. Do you hear me!"

"ZZZr ZZZng ZZZaws ZZZr ZZZee."

"What! What did you say!" Paul came within a centimeter of Floyd's disgusting countenance, screaming, saliva coating his thin lips. Floyd's walleyes flashed this way and that as he shook his head from side to side. Yet I could tell, even Floyd was intimidated and humiliated this time.

And he sat there all day. But then, miraculously, when all the lunch trays were cleared and the clients restored to their post-lunch torpor, Floyd had disappeared. The three of us, Kelvin, Dorothy, and I noticed it simultaneously. The white, blue-trimmed posey all twisted and limp lay loudly in the yellow high-backed chair. We all thought the same thing. We should find him immediately and return him to his spot before Paul found out. But before we could even communicate that singular idea to each other, the wicked witch of the west walked into the room. He saw it immediately, and we all stood back to watch the steam spew out of his ears. And just as Paul seemed ready to explode, sweet little Merry Mary came running into the room from the exit door a little bit out of breath:

"Paul, Floyd just went poopy on the stairs, I saw him."

Well, I've never seen such a transformation of facial sentiment in all my life—except maybe that time John Brown pulled his teeth out of his head and his face fell down. Paul, who'd been in a self-inflicted pressure cooker all day, suddenly began to float above the floor with ethereal bouyancy. The swollen red, grimacing face popped. He began to glow, smiling beatifically.

"Floyd, Floyd, Floyd," he tisked, tisked, tisked happily on his way over to the intercom. "Gloria! Oh Gloria!" he called gayly as he pressed the intercom button.

"Yes Paul," the forced professional tone with the grating nasalization came over the speaker.

"Please come up to the third floor. I have something interesting to tell you."

"What is it?"

"It's a surprise, he he he," and he giggled. Then he hung up and turned immediately around to us, snapping his fingers. "Kelvin, get a bucket and mop and go clean up that mess. Richard, find Floyd," this was all said quite contumeliously with glaring racist overtones.

Poor Floyd, he knew his goose was cooked the minute Merry Mary saw him. I had a hell of a time finding him. In fact, I didn't. The cook downstairs found him a half-hour later when he noticed a bright pair of white sneakers sticking out from under the refrigerator in the kitchen.

The day the Sheriff and his deputy escorted Floyd away was a dark day for me. I had always romanticized about Floyd. He was a modern-day hero in my eyes. I was his greatest fan. He was my inspiration. But seeing him there that day a little pitiful bug wedged helplessly between those two huge men reeking of the sane society outside made me realize that there was no game playing allowed in this world, no game playing at all.

leslie's story

A nurse's aide, especially in a bughouse, is the last word in the service industry. There's nothing you don't do for the client. You shave him, floss his teeth, pick his nose, arrest his dandruff, remove his eye gunk, dewax his ears, clip his toenails, wipe his ass, etc. In essence, the madman is the nurse's aide's very own baby, and no matter if you're man or woman, you respond to that call like a mother goose.

The reason I mention this is because Leslie Wilder was the maddest of them all and needed plenty of servicing. He was so mad, in fact, that if you left him to his own devices he would wound himself beyond repair. He liked digging sharp things into his skin, especially his fingernails, so you had to stay on top of those. Because of this he always had some nasty, festering sore on his person. He also hated clothes and would rip and tear and flush his down the toilet. He did this constantly so that at the end of each day his clothes had to be hidden from him. But it was a losing battle, and each week we had to buy him another shirt, another pair of shoes, pants or underwear. Many times I found him traipsing through the halls in his birthday suit. He liked to fondle himself, too, or he liked penises in general. Perhaps that's what did him in.

One thing that separated me from the rest of the aides besides my complexion and background was that I read the clients' files. We had access to them, which I considered a great privilege. Whenever things were slow, I'd grab a file and read. What I found out right off was that the famous axiom "every man has a story to tell" is certainly true for the madman, the only difference being that the madman's story is his own indictment. This indictment, after it has been edited, rewritten, expanded upon, analyzed, criticized, and then rubber-stamped, reads like the synopsis of a great screen play. It has a compelling storyline with a neat beginning, middle, and end. And, nine times out of ten, this cosmological chronicle of insanity ends with a Bang!

Leslie was an only child born to a schizophrenic mother who killed herself when Leslie was quite young. She hanged herself with an electrical cord and was swinging to and fro from the rafters in the garage when Leslie came home from school. Poor Leslie never got along well with his peers. He was quiet and distant and inclined to be cruel to animals. Many accounts were recorded by teachers and neighbors and family members of Leslie ceremoniously executing helpless fauna. Leslie's IQ was found to be a whopping 150. He had a penchant for poetry and read a great deal, especially Shakespeare. In high school he became involved in theater and was quickly recognized as an unmitigated talent.

But Leslie hung around the wrong people in the wrong places at the wrong hours. He seduced a young boy of twelve in the neighborhood and was caught. He was held up for public ridicule which affected him greatly. Shortly thereafter he dropped out of school, just weeks before his graduation, and took a job as an usher in a movie theater. He held this job for two years. During this period he was arrested several times for solicitation in public restrooms, once in fact, at the movie theater itself.

Always a lover of the dramatic arts, Leslie decided to go to

Hollywood. Borrowing most of the money from his father, he bought a car and some new clothes and drove the two thousand miles from his home in suburban Chicago to the Land of Dreams. In Hollywood, he found a room at a motel and headed directly to the home of a well-known actor. Within the week he proved himself to be quite a nuisance to the famed star, and on one occasion had to be escorted off the private property by the police. Exactly one month from the day that he had arrived in Hollywood, Leslie Wilder was arrested by the Beverly Hills police for breaking and entering, indecent exposure, and a half dozen other violations. He had, apparently, managed to enter the home of this matinee idol via a basement window. When the man came home he found, to his surprise, Leslie Wilder spread out buck naked across his bed. The police held him for two weeks, but charges were dropped when Leslie promised to leave town upon his release and he was set free.

Three days later his father came home to find him inside urinating in the basement with only a T-shirt on. The father summoned the men with the white coats.

Leslie, by the time I met him, had been institutionalized for over thirty years. He was a mess, as I said, but he was friendly and if you asked him to do something he would try to oblige you. Occasionally, I would have to go down and retrieve him from the second floor where the adolescents were accomodated. He liked to show some of the boys his penis. But it was innocent fun because Leslie was quite heavily medicated. So, around and around and around the halls he'd go in his ill-fitting clothes, wearing shirts with all the buttons ripped off, with scratches on his arms and chest and face, and all the while mumbling a few choice lines.

His genius, or his theatrical comportment I should say, was never more evident than when Doctor Comfort, the doddering female psychiatrist, came to counsel the clients. God knows how long that charade had been going on:

DOCTOR COMFORT: Hello, Leslie.

LESLIE WILDER: Hello.

DOCTOR COMFORT: Talk to me Leslie. How are you doing?

LESLIE WILDER: Fine. I must employ you in some business against our nuptial, I might add.

DOCTOR COMFORT: Leslie! You're acting again. Why do you put on this act? You want to act crazy, it's easier for you, isn't it? Acting crazy is easier than acting sane, isn't it Leslie?

LESLIE WILDER: (Leslie opens his mouth to say something, but only yawns and sits back in his chair looking recondite.)

DOCTOR COMFORT: It's all just an act, isn't it Leslie?

LESLIE WILDER: All the world's a stage. (shrugging smugly)

DOCTOR COMFORT: Why don't we try something new. Why don't you try acting sane, how about that? Why don't you try acting like you were normal and happy. Do you think you can do that? Dress nicely, say nice things to people, should we try that?

LESLIE WILDER: That? Well, your plaintain leaf is excellent for that.

DOCTOR COMFORT: Leslie! Sane! Let's act sane from now on, should we try it? Let's. No quotes from Shakespeare, no pants flushed down the toilet, no ripping buttons off our shirts, no scratching ourselves. Sane. Say nice things. Should we try it?

LESLIE WILDER: Sane?

DOCTOR COMFORT: Yes, Leslie. Let's play that part from now on.

LESLIE WILDER: Ha ha ha ha. That part. (His laugh is theatrical.)

DOCTOR COMFORT: There's nothing funny about it, Leslie. You can do it, I know you can. It's hard, but you can do it because you're a great actor. You can play any part, but this time let's stick to one character—a normal, sane, nice, well-groomed, middle-aged man. Shall we try?"

LESLIE WILDER: (He scratches his crew cut head and screws up his face.) Okay.

DOCTOR COMFORT: You can go.

LESLIE WILDER: (Leslie starts to walk away, but then turns suddenly back to Doctor Comfort with a frightened look.) The body is with the king, but the king is not with the body. The king is a thing!

DOCTOR COMFORT: Sane, Leslie!

LESLIE WILDER: Sane? (Scratching himself viciously, then a light bulb of inspiration alights his face.) I see a cherub that sees them. But, come, for England. Farewell dear mother.

(Exeunt)

I used to fantasize that some day a famous director would find out about Leslie and come and steal him away, then dress him in theatrical wardrobe and put him up on stage as the Prince of Denmark. I was convinced that he'd give the performance of the century. I could just see him . . . as the stage lights began to heat up and cause him a little discomfort, Leslie would begin to disrobe so that by the end of Act III there'd be a naked Hamlet prancing madly about on stage, mortifying his flesh and pissing all over the props. Like I said, the performance of the century.

ole jake's taboo

Without a doubt the most fitting metaphor of all is the broken record. The lunatic, for the most part, is possessed by a singular notion or image—an idée fixe to use a French phrase. Yes, perhaps there is a chemical imbalance which triggers the whole damn thing, but I can tell you this: something happens to a person, a trauma, a disappointment, a fear that takes hold of his brain—his record if you will—and scratches the shit out of it.

Ole Jake, bowlegged as a cowboy, sat outside his room and greeted everyone who walked by:

"Howdydoo, howdydoo," he'd say convivially.

He was an old man, eighty years old, and in good health for eighty. He'd shuffle around the place, head down, moving about with apparent purpose. In fact, if you didn't work there on the floor and you weren't familiar with the people, you might, after being greeted by Ole Jake or watching him walk about, ask yourself what he was doing in such a place. And if you went up to him and talked with him just for a minute or so, he'd definitely convince you that he had no reason to be there.

"It's a fuckin' bughouse," he'd say. "A goddamn bughouse. I should have walked out of here when I had the chance forty years ago.

"Now what am I gonna do? Who's gonna hire an old man

eighty years old? They treat me like I'm goddamn crazy. I ain't crazy, goddamn it. I could walk the hell out this door right now and they couldn't stop me. But where am I gonna go—eighty years old?"

Of course this was repeated daily, twice, thrice, four times . . . This broken record was yelled full vibrato in my face whenever I had to remind him of his self-care responsibilities because he forgot a lot.

"Jake, it's your bath day. Here's some soap and a towel. I put a razor on the edge of the bathtub for you."

Two seconds before, he was smiling cordially at me, but that smile quickly disintegrated into a look of complete disgust as soon as I started to accost him.

"Goddamn it I ain't crazy! You treat me like I'm crazy or something. I ain't nuts. This fuckin' bughouse. I should have walked the hell out of here when I had the chance forty years ago . . . "

"Take the towel, Jake."

"Who's gonna hire an old man eighty years old? I could walk out this door right now and you couldn't stop me!"

"Here Jake, just take the soap and towel, please."

"Where the hell am I gonna go? Eighty years old, where the hell am I gonna go?" accusatorily.

About at this point he'd usually acquiesce and take the towel and the soap with a menacing glance and shuffle to his task.

There was more to the broken record of course. These oft repeated lines were merely the effect of scratches made many many years before. So long ago that no one really knew when it all happened. And of all the people there, he was the only one who was self-committed.

"Paul say he been institutionalize' the longes' of anyone, Richud. He commit hisself ya know. Been institutionalize' fifty years at leas'," Dorothy informed.

I tend to doubt that there is any inherent sympathy or compassion in man. I believe there is only pity and empathy.

And I find nothing wrong with pity. In fact, I think we're all such pitiful creatures that pity is an exclusively human condition. Ole Jake's story was the quintessence of pitiful. I came upon it quite innocently, without having to nose around in his files. Same scene as before—trying to get him to bathe—when I finally, out of impatience, asked him why he didn't just up and walk the hell out the door when he had the chance forty years before.

"What's that?"

"You keep sayin' you should have walked out of here forty years ago. Why didn't you?"

His pissed-off look suddenly turned sheepish. "She ruined me, that's why. She made an absolute fool out of me. They laughed at me everywhere I went. Couldn't even walk into my office without them laughing behind my back. It didn't matter, wherever I went they laughed. Runnin' around with her own goddamn brother!"

"What? Who?" I was instantly confused.

"My wife, that's who, who do you think? Greek slut. She was runnin' around with her own goddamn brother and everybody knew it, too. Everybody but me. Even the boss knew. I had a good job—"

"You mean her step-brother?" Still scratching my head.

"No, goddamn it, I mean her brother. Greeks. Made a fool out of me. Lost my job. They laughed at me everywhere I went. Made an absolute fool out of me. Runnin' around with her own goddamn brother. They do that, those Greeks . . ."

When I told Dorothy later that day what Ole Jake had let slip, she only shook her head in pity.

"Ain' it the wors' story you ever hear? I never heard nothin' like it befo'."

It was her comment that jarred something loose in me and made me realize something we all must know intrinsically—like Oedipus or Electra or Adam and Eve—breaking a taboo is certain doom.

saint nick

Nick's monthly visits had a profound effect on all of us. He would cut the men's hair on the third floor one month, and the next month the boys' hair down on the second floor, so I'd seen him on the job only twice.

There was something—and I am not at all inclined to use such a word—divine about Nick's presence amongst them. Even Dorothy, the guardian mother, deferred in spirit to Nick. It was like he expired all the missing molecules which they, like suffocating plants, greedily respired. Where Dorothy sustained and nurtured, he gave new hope, new life. No question, Nick was a saint.

So there he stood, scissors at the ready, a head in position below his chin; those rosy red cheeks; that soft, bald-headed glow; and in those olive eyes just one singular sentiment—love for his fellow man. In those sweet, mild eyes there existed no judgment, no prejudice, no disagreement. Wherever he was, whomever he met, everyone in his ken was equal, every man jack of us. There was no difference between me and Bobby, for instance, or between Cap'n John and the King of Spain for that matter. We were all "his'a buddies; his'a young fellas."

He, like all mystics, had the power to tame the most savage breast. Floyd, Leslie Wilder, Fred, Megs, Bobby—they were all putty in his hands. He snipped away at their hair, talking all the while, getting them to smile, to say a few coherent words, and then sending them on their way with a handshake and a pat on the shoulder. In those fifteen minutes in his charge, it was amazing to see the effect he had on each of them. And never, never, was that hackneyed expression more fitting upon the completion of a haircut—"Like a new man."

Of course he could talk a blue streak, that was part of his power. In retrospect those stories he told weren't just stories, they were lessons, parables, case in point: "Beppe an'a dee Queena Sophia."

"Hey my buddy, how'a you doin' today? Wanna nice'a haircut? Look good for dee dance? Sure, sit'a right down, make'a youself comfort'ble, Nick take'a good care you," he'd say as one of the clients would sit in his chair. He'd toss up that apron like pizza dough, and let it float down onto his customer like a magic spell.

"They'a treatin' you nice here? No complain's? Good, good. Get plenty food, nice'a warm bat's you take, lot nice people to take care you. 'At's'a my buddy. Stay out'a trouble, do what'a these nice peoples say. They'a you frien's, wanna do what's best for you." Then he'd tell a story: "Now when I gotta married, my wife she do ev'ryt'ing for me. Ev'ryt'ing! Getta my clothes clean, make'a dee food, fresh fish, meat, iron, press dee shirts, ev'ryt'ing'a nice, jus'a dee way it suppose'a be. Now, at'a that time, I no like alla that because I live by myself for'a ten years before she come 'long. I was use take'a care myself. This in Italy long'a time 'go. I come home an'a ev'ryt'ing jus'a right. I get alla grumpy, wanna wear my T-shirt, like a little mess around me like'a I was use to. But I no tell'a dee wife 'cause I know she no un'erstan' me, see, I jus'a keep to myself, an'a ev'rytime I come home I make a leedle mess. Then one day I come home'a from work an'a find dee whole house a mess. Clo'es ev'rywhere, glasses, newspapers ev'rywhere. 'Madonna' I says to myself, what'a happen here? It look'a like garbage'a dump. I look 'round for my wife an' dere she is on'a dee bed, cryin'. I sit down next her an'a ask her what'a she cryin' 'bout, what'a happen. She say she try to make'a dee house jus'a dee way I like it, but she don' feel right for what she done. I begin to laugh. She done all dat mess for me because she notice I don'a like t'ings jus'a right. Ha ha, she a good lady. So from then on I never do nothin' to make a mess. She wanna make'a me happy, an' I wanna make'a her happy, too. So today, t'irtya-five years later, we still happy."

He must have told a hundred stories just like that one, never the same, but always with a message at the end.

"My wife, what dee firs' place she wanna see when she move to America? Montecarlo in Virginia. She read all 'bout Tomasso Jefferason in school. She always talkin' 'bout Tomasso Jefferason dis, Tomasso Jefferason dat. She know all there is to know about dee guy. So dee firs' vacation time I get, we go down to Montecarlo. We take our time, drive'a down, look at all dee sights—Washington D.C., Williamsatown an'a Jamesatown, the Blue Ridge Mountain Drive. Che bello! Beautiful. May, ev'ryat'ing green. Then we go to Montecarlo. Up, up'a dee hill we drive. He pick out a nice'a high spot for himself, that guy. An'a we walk 'roun' an'a 'roun' dee house, dee gardens, dee gif' shop. My wife, she'a speechless. She say it jus' like dee way she see it in'a her head from all dee books she read. We dere all day. Take'a dee tour of dee house tree times. She no wanna go. I tell'a her we gotta go, it'a late, we gotta get back home. She still no wanna go. So I pick her up an'a put her in dee car. Che lacrime! She start to cry. Big'a tears like my thumbs rollin' down'a her cheeks. She'a cryin', people lookin', wonderin'. Gesu Maria! Then I see someat'ing—get'a idea; stop'a dee car. Over next dee driveway there's bed pachysandra. Now my wife, she gotta green thumb. Plants ev'rywhere you come to my house. So I get out'a dee car, open'a dee trunk an' get a old coffee can. At's'a right, coffee can. What I do, see, is dig up'a dee pachysandra and put it in'a dee can. She stop cryin' and start to smile. She un'erstan' what'a I doin'. See, I was takin' dee pachysandra for her garden. Not takin' 'xactly, jus'a borrowin'. I figure Mr. Jefferason, he'a nice man, if he was'a there, wouldn't a mind. I get back in dee car and she give me a big kiss on dee cheek. Now anyone come to dee house, firs'a t'ing she show them is dee pachysandra from Tomasso Jefferason house, Montecarlo."

All day long, story after story. And all day long, there I'd stand loyally listening to every word, laughing and responding when propriety demanded.

That day after he was finished we stood at the exit door and shook hands before he left. He just winked, smiled, and said, "'At's'a nice'a white shirt, buddy. My wife, she'a make it whiter for you, you want."

mon cheri

Pouvre, petite Mon Cheri. She paced around all day in a circle, pointing at the ceiling with the index finger of her right hand while the fingers of the left hand twitched and twirled out in front of her like eels or like a group of tiny beings conversing among themselves. She moaned a lot. She was a tortured soul. Sometimes she would break down and start crying buckets right there on the floor. We would have to pick her up and carry her to bed. Other times we would find her in bed curled up in the fetal position, moaning quietly to herself. We could do nothing for her. She'd stay that way for days. And yet, despite all of her suffering, she still said hello to me every day she saw me. And she smiled. Oh what a smile she had!

Mon Cheri looked like a cabbage patch doll. In fact, of all the people there, I would have to say that she was the one I would least want to run into in a dark alley. Her features were so unreal—her round little head, her button-like eyes, her lipless mouth, her meaty nostrilless nose. . . . And yet despite all of these goulish aspects, you automatically loved her. It was her will that shined through it all. It was her will that smiled at you.

I could easily have choked Gloria to death without any feelings of remorse. We all know thousands of people, each one of us, and to say that just a handful of them we could kill without remorse is, perhaps, not such a shocking reality. Gloria walked in on Mon Cheri when she was in one of her fetal funks. She came back out into the hall with those white-woman no-lips of hers pursed, her inspid blue eyes beady and sinister, her rat-like snout twitching—

"How long has she been like that?" she demanded from Dorothy.

"Jus' a day. She come out of it soon."

"That's passive aggressive behavior. I want you to document every time she does that."

"She fine, she jus' un'er the weather's all."

"You document these fits, do you understand! Passive aggressive is unacceptable behavior here!"

Gloria needed to be choked 'til her whole body was bright blue. She wanted Mon Cheri out because she knew how bad it looked when she took to her bed like that. Her tours, her little tours with the potential clients' families, were all that she ever thought about. As if Mon Cheri taking to her bed like that looked any worse than Leslie Wilder parading around nude with scratches all over his face, or Bobby sitting there bawling, or Fred sleeping with his spoonful of food stuck halfway up to his mouth, or Mount Shirley erupting. . . . Everything and everybody looked bad. Which of course was the point of the place, Jesus Christ! And to have Gloria constantly walking around to point out all these "unsightly" aspects made you just want to grab her by the neck and squeeze, squeeze, squeeze the pitiful life out of her.

"Passive aggressive? What that s'pose' to mean?" Dorothy asked me when Gloria walked away, her eyes squinting painfully, her rational mind whispering to her about how fucked up and nonsensical is Whitemanspeak.

"It's an oxymoron." Adding more fuel to the fire.

"Now whatchu sayin', chile?"

"Nothin', that's what it means. A positive and a negative equals zero. It means nothing."

"Tha's what I thought," she nodded proudly, walking away satisfied.

Mon Cheri didn't want to be the way she was, which is what upset her so. That discontent was what sent her to bed. She was so tortured and yet so strong at the same time. Any normal person would have done away with herself long before. But Mon Cheri fought and fought and fought. I felt it was the most internecine battle I'd ever seen or ever would see. The ultimate battle, really, a Jobian battle. It was conditioning versus free will. And whatever the conditioning was, her free will sure didn't agree with it. Free will had to be a fifteen-to-one long shot. Conditioning bullies us all. Mr. Humanity himself, B. F. Skinner, would have shaken his mighty head at the uselessness of the struggle. But Krishnamurti, on Mon Cheri's other shoulder, would have looked on approvingly at one engaged in such a noble battle.

Dorothy never documented a single episode of Mon Cheri's fits. We let the battle continue. Mon Cheri's smile never faded.

m e ġ s

Megs was Kelvin's dog. This is a cruel way to describe him but to all intents and purposes he was. He followed Kelvin wherever he went, shuffling along, never picking up his feet, with his big lips crookedly unfurled on his face. His eyes were severely cataracted and this gave him a ghostly appearance because, upon looking him in the eye, one saw no color, no cognizance, no glow of presence of mind. He was a little man in his early eighties, no more than five feet four, with unproportionately long arms and leg-of-mutton hands. His shoulders were surprisingly square, and without a shirt on he still cut an imposing figure. He was bent a little to his right because he possessed greater power and density on that side, and gravity conspired to distend him like that. He had cauliflower ear, heavily scarred brows, and a smashed-in nose. This was because he had been a boxer. He couldn't have been much more than a featherweight.

Contrary to all the other clients' files, Megs' was sorely incomplete. It mentions only that he was from New York, that he was a boxer, and that he was diagnosed with Alzheimer's, but that's it. No details. I even went to the public library and searched through microfilm files of the *New York Times* from sixty years ago to see if I could find his name in the fight columns. I found nothing, but I'm sure he didn't fight under his real name—Guido Meglioni. I prodded him for months about his nom de pug, but there was no way he could process that kind of a question. Anyway, he was the undisputed champion of the Rainbow House.

Megs was Fred's roommate, and before I came on the scene, Kelvin was getting them both up in the morning. That was my very first assignment, in fact. It is emblazened in my frontal lobes forever because that was my very first impression of the place.

On that first morning, Dorothy met me as I stood alone looking around in the big day room. She greeted me with the charm of an angel and then brought me over to Fred and Meg's room and pointed at the closed door.

"Kelvin be in there, Richud. He gettin' the mens dress'. You jus' go in there and he show you what to do."

I walked uneasily into the room. There was a radio on the window ledge at the far side of the room playing a loud, insolent rap song. Below the window was a bed with Fred's big white, naked body on it, the sheets pulled off of him. His back was to me and he was snoring despite the obnoxious music. To my immediate right was a door. There were muffled voices behind it; I took a step towards it and leaned closer to hear—

"Honey, that's not nice, what would yo' mamma think?"

"MUH MUH MUH MY MOTHER! WUH WUH WUH WHAT'RE YOU SAYIN' ABOUT MY MOTHER!"

"Nothin' cousin, nothin', jus' calm down." It was quiet for a few moments. "You know, I won' even mention all that cocksuckin' she done."

"Oh, okay." There was silence. "WUH WUH WUH WHAT DID YOU SAY! COCKSUCKER! WHO YOU CALLIN' A COCKSUCKER!" Then there was the sound of a scuffle, though Kelvin's giggling communicated the dynamics of it.

At this point I knocked diffidently on the door.

"See cousin, here yo' mother now." The door slowly opened revealing Kelvin and Megs, the latter was stationed on the toilet staring straight ahead into oblivion. "You the new aide?"

"Yeah," I croaked.

"I'm Kelvin." We shook the brother shake. "Hey, awright. This is Megs." We both looked down on the old man staring vacantly at the wall in front of him. "He got the Ole Timer's bad. You cain' leave him 'lone or he punch the other clients. He Eyetalian. You Eyetalian?" eyeing me suspiciously.

"Half."

"Oh. Anyway, he use' to be a boxer. Don' put yo' face in fron' o' him o' he bang you one. An don' be callin' him no cocksucker o' he—"

"WUH WUH WUH WHAD YOU CALL ME?" Megs shouted, rising from the toilet seat.

"See what I mean. You a han'some dude, cousin, that's what we say."

"Oh." And he sat back down, his expression blank as a statue.

"An' don' say nothin' 'bout his mother o' he really get excited."

"MUH MUH MUH MY MOTHER!" he stuttered, rising from the toilet seat again.

"Whad I tell ya," Kelvin nodded to me. Then to Megs: "She a nice lady."

"Oh."

As young men will do, especially idle young men working side by side in a loony bin, we made a competition of Megs. We would sit him down on the toilet seat or on his bed and then, one at a time, we'd put our face in front of his and call him a cocksucker or say something blasphemous about his mother. We'd see who could block and parry and duck under the most punches. Actually, this was Kelvin's game before I came along, he just had the good fortune to be able to share it with a pal.

He usually won, but then he had six years experience on me.

So Megs would follow Kelvin around all day, shuffling along in that simian gait. Kelvin had to feed him too, because he coudn't remember long enough to eat what was in front of him. Megs was very loving and thankful. It was funny to watch and listen to those two at breakfast or lunch:

"Open up honey," holding a spoonful of oatmeal.

"Ahhhhhh . . . (opening wide, then biting down on the entering spoon, swishing the gruel around his mouth and finally swallowing). Th-th-th-thank you, honey."

"My pleasure, cousin."

"Ha ha ha ha, you're a n-n-n-nice guy."

"You a sweet guy, too, you know that. Open up."

"Ahhhhhhh . . . (opening wide, then biting down on the entering spoon, swishing the gruel around his mouth and finally swallowing). Th-th-th-thank you, you're a nice guy."

"You jus' sayin' that. Open up."

"Ahhhhhh . . . (opening wide, then biting down on the entering spoon, swishing the gruel around his mouth and finally swallowing). Th-th-th-thank you."

"You welcome, cocksucker. Open up."

"AhhhhhhWUH WUH WUH . . . " (beginning to rise, avoiding the offered spoon).

"Shhhh, honey, you a great guy. Now open up."

"Ahhhhhhh . . . (sitting down, smiling and opening his mouth, then biting down on the entering spoon, swishing the gruel around his mouth and finally swallowing). Th-th-th-thank you, honey."

"Don' mention it. Open up."

"Ahhhhhhh . . . "

"Tha's it now, keep it open, jus' like yo' mamma use' to do when them weenies was comin' in."

"AhhhhhhhhMUH MUH MUH MY MOTHER!"

Etc.

Without Kelvin, Megs would have been shipped out the moment the new owner bought the place. See, you couldn't leave Megs alone with the rest of the clients even for a minute or he'd blast them. Occasionally, Kelvin would let him wander around by his lonesome just to see what would happen. We'd sit back and watch the disaster unfold. He'd want to talk with people and he'd shuffle after them calling—"Huh-huh-huh-honey! Huh-huh-huh-honey!" And he'd want to put his nose in their face. As soon as one of them obliged him, we'd jump to his side and catch his arms just in the nick of time. Then one day we weren't able to catch him. That was the end of him, that was the last punch he'd ever throw at the Rainbow. But, I must admit, he couldn't have chosen a better punch to throw at a more deserving head.

It was late afternoon and Diane, the recreation aide, was conducting her weekly dance class on the floor. She had her tape player going and it was cranking out some old-time waltz music. Suddenly there was a disturbance. The Alzheimer's lady, Amelia, who had been waltzing quite continentally with one of the male schizophrenic clients, just up and kicked him right in the groin. This man went down like a ton of bricks, and Kelvin and I ran to his aid. Just at this exact moment, who should come sashaying onto the floor conducting one of her obnoxious tours for the relatives of a prospective client, but rat-like Gloria with her piercingly squeaky and nasalized voice. She stopped in her tracks and looked down in disgust at Kelvin and me on hands and knees attending to the stricken schizoid.

"What happened?" she frowned.

"Amelia kick him," Kelvin growled.

"Tsss," she smacked her tongue loudly against the roof of her mouth and expelled air at the same time, expressing her disgust.

Kelvin and I were in the process of leading the man over to a chair when we both heard the tell-tale squeak—

"And how are you today, Mr. Meglioni?"

Our necks snapped around in unison just in time to see Megs, nose to nose with Gloria, pivot his weight from his right hip into his right fist, which, with blurring speed, cut an arc across his midsection and streaked down through the point of Gloria's shiny chin. It was a picture-perfect hook, like the Frazier left in Ali/Frazier I. She went down in a heap, lights out for a good ten minutes. What a punch!

The Sheriff's Department came a couple of days later to escort him to the County. Gloria appeared back at work a week after that wearing a neck brace. Poor Megs, he's in a locked ward somewhere without anyone to call him a cocksucker. I get a lump in my throat just thinking about it.

cootie, the hoodoo man

Cootie walked on the ceiling, so-to-speak—everyone looked up to him. That's because he had a job. A job! He worked on a farm during the day and received a paycheck once a month for his labors. Everyone admired him. When he left for work in the morning, all heads would turn, all eyes would follow the boogagloo beat of his feet as he shuffled out the exit door and down the stairs to a waiting van. A job! And at the end of the day, upon his return, a dozen of the exact same questions would assault him as he walked back through the door—"How was work today, Cootie?" He'd mumble some Mumbo Jumbo and shuffle into the hopper. The whole roost would ruffle its feathers and coo. He was the resident hero.

Cootie was a paranoid, about forty years old. He was black as black could be, New Orleans black, with big puckered-out lips, protruding brow bones, and a mojo han'. He jerked and bobbed along on the heels of his leather shoes, his hands jammed down deep into his pockets, moving his head forward and back as he locomoted like a chicken with rhythm. He was about five feet six, a sinewy 140 pounds, with broad shoulders and a tiny waist. He didn't like company, like a true paranoid. In fact, if you crowded him he'd just slip you the mojo han' and skeedaddle. He spoke an incomprehensible dialect that only Dorothy could follow. He'd shuffle around the place, mumbling Mumbo Jumbo to himself in what I considered the blackest Black English of them all. But it was lyrical. And if you listened real close, you might catch a few phrases, might hear him describing his day at work in rhyming slang:

> "Ah axed da boss ta lea' me work da hog fo' a while;
> Ta clea' da hay n' skat befo' dem pocras ge' back.
> An soo' dey do, ah heb ta run ta pu' da fodra dow',
> An' cross da sty ta watch 'em set dow' 'n chow.
> Dey aw bu' shoat, 'bou' fity poun' no mo'.
> Sho' be growin' fas', growin' fas' like wee' 'na grass . . . "

Dorothy used to tease him. She could speak a little of the hoodoo language—born in the Mississippi Delta herself. She'd push Cootie into a corner and want to see his mojo han'—

"W'chu got? Lemme see. Sho' it to me," giggling; Cootie all serious.

"I hoodoo you. You hoodooed now. Ain' nothin' but I co' do," he'd flash the hand then jam it back deep into his pocket.

"You cain' do dat. I got the Lawd Jesus on my shoulder, chile. He don' stan' fo' no hoodooin'." Dorothy'd turn around with her huge gold-toothed smile and flash it at me and worm her finger for me to join her—she knew I was into it. I'd come in for a closer look-see and Cootie'd really get his mojo working—

"Who he? I hoodoo him too."

"Dis sweet why' chile?" Dorothy would grab me by the hand and pull me to her side. We'd stand over Cootie, waiting for the hand to flash. "He got da rabbi's fo' 'na pockeh," Dorothy would warn, holding back a giggle. "Besi', he ain' afraid a no hoodoo coon."

"Don' caw me dat." Then it would flash for an instant from out of the pocket like a snake striking from the tall grass. "He hoodooed now. He done hoodooed." And off he'd shuffle, the mojo han' coiled deep inside his pocket.

I admired Cootie, too, just like the rest of them. I looked up when he came in from his day's work, and I looked after him with fatherly pride as he walked out the exit door in the morning. I glowed like the rest of them when he'd get that monthly check handed to him in the mail. And I, too, would gloat at the sight of him as he counted, in merry Mumbo Jumbo, the four crisp hundred-dollar bills he'd get after cashing the check. And sometimes, if I got real close, I could hear the lyrical tune of how the money would work—

"A hunred go fo' a wris' wach, gol' cara';
Notha hun'red fo' shoes, nice new pair;
Pu' a hun'red 'na bank, keepena safe place;
Leeb da res' fo' ma pockeh, spen' i' 'notha day."

mount shirley

At least once a day Mount Shirley erupted. There was no usual time. She'd just be sitting there quietly working that cigarette for all it was worth with her dark, flaming eyes fixed onto a spot; her brown, gray-streaked hair all stringy and oily; her tar-stained and tremulous fingers poised with the cigarette in front of her toothless maw dreaming up wicked thoughts. Suddenly, like a Jack in the Box, she'd vault to her feet and let us all have it.

Shirley was a dyed-in-the-wool paranoid, but the scary thing about Shirley was that she was omniscient. She knew every-thing about everyone and she'd let us know it too. She'd stand up there spewing fire, the unfallacious philippics recited quickly and glibly without any hestitation:

Re Bobby: "Look at him! He's a baby. He has no teeth! Do you want to suck my titty, baby? How pitiful! Listen to him cry. Just like a shitassed baby! Where's your mommy, baby? He's disgusting."

Re Megs: "Look at him sitting there! He doesn't know where he is. He doesn't even know his own name! He has no mind left!"

Re Leslie: "Look at Laurence Olivier over there! Oh he thinks he's so theatrical, but he can't even tie his own shoes.

He's insane! He's queer, too, with his feminine eyes. He sickens me."

Re Amelia: "She plays the great lady, but she shits in her pants and pees in her bed. She's not fooling anyone; her husband was a plumber. Look at her pretending! She makes me sick!"

Re John Brown: "He's worried about his mother all day long, but she never comes to see him. She doesn't want to see him. She doesn't want to be reminded that she gave birth to a creature."

Re Eulalia: "What a witch! What a nothing person. Look at her with her broom and her hair like that! Keep sweepin' witch! Everyone's dirty but her. Slut! She'll screw anything that moves. I hate her."

Re Ole Jake: "He should have walked out the door forty years ago when he had the chance. Ha ha ha, who's he kidding, he's the sickest bastard in the place. Thinks the whole world knows about his wife. Thinks the whole world's laughing behind his back. Well he's right, including me—Ha ha ha . . . "

Re Floyd: "Oh he's ridiculous! He's so insignificant. He thinks we're all worried about what he's going to do next. We couldn't care less. Why don't you jump out the window. That might get our attention."

Re Cootie: "He thinks he's a witch doctor, got special powers. He's just a dumb spook. He can't even talk right, his lips are too big. He's nuts! Why don't you stay at the farm, sleep with the pigs where you belong!"

Re Kelvin: "He thinks he's so cool, but what's he doing working here? He's just like the rest of his family, afraid to take a chance. Get a real job. I can't stand him."

Re Me: "He doesn't belong here! What the hell is he doing here!"

Re Paul: "Nobody likes him, 'specially himself. He loves controlling us with his pills. He lives for that. That's the only control he has over his life. Look at him! Go ahead, give me another pill, I know it makes you feel better. Cocksucker!"

She actually never would get to caluminate more than two or three clients or staff at a time because Paul was on her in a flash. In fact, there was something uncanny about Paul's quick appearance whenever Shirley would erupt. I wouldn't see Paul all day, but if I was nearby when Shirley let loose, Paul would appear as if by magic with a plastic cup in one hand and a pink pill in the other. I figured it had to do with her insults regarding his sexuality, or that he simply didn't want the other clients to be subjected to such abuse. In any case, Shirley would have been the first one out the door when the new administration began its purge if it hadn't been for Paul and his promptness. Just one of those pills and Shirley was a dormant volcano for another day.

But then one day I found out the real reason for Paul's exceptional treatment of Shirley. I was wrong in both of my conjectures—Shirley was Paul's ace in the hole, so to speak.

Paul had always felt threatened in his job. He knew it hinged on his ability to document and corroborate grounds for removal. Well, a couple of months had gone by without a single soul being bumped over to the County. The administration was anxious and leaning pretty hard on the nurses; a few had even been fired. Paul felt the heat and threw down his ace.

I noticed almost from the very first that Paul was allowing Shirley to rant and rave for much longer than usual. In the past, it couldn't have been longer than two minutes before he was in front of her with the little plastic cup of water and the pink pill. It was all too apparent when Shirley's leash was let out. Five, ten, sometimes as long as fifteen minutes Shirley would be there, on fire, her eyes glowing fire, her voice growing hoarse, letting everyone in her ken have it on the kisser. Paul would eventually appear looking annoyed, looking like he'd become utterly disgusted with Shirley.

I remember the comment the all-knowing Dorothy made to me after watching Paul arrive ten minutes late with Shirley's muzzle pill: "She all done now, Richud. You watch, Paul been savin' her to make hisself look good."

Sure enough, two weeks later Doctor Comfort arrived on the scene with her cane and crispy complexion. Her entrance was the usual parade of professionals, with Gloria, the little vermin, buzzing around her in double-time. They collected Shirley and sat her down alone on one side of the long dining tables, while they all sat in front of her on the other side—Dr. Comfort, Paul, Gloria, and the social worker. Dorothy and I looked on from across the room, pretending to be taking clients' vital signs. We both realized right away that Shirley had not been medicated. It was the greatest eruption since Krakatau, east of Java.

Dr. Comfort: "Paul tells us you've been quite angry lately, Shirley."

Shirley: Sits staring hatefully at her accusers, her dark, smoldering eyes wide, her toothless maw sucking in on a cigarette.

Dr. Comfort: "Shirley, are you angry?"

Shirely: "Oh shut up! What do you care!"

Dr. Comfort: "Shirley, Paul tells us—"

Shirley: "Paul? Fuck Paul! Paul can go to hell! He's such a weak person. He hates his job, he hates himself, and he hates his father! I'll tell you what Paul is . . . !" Shirley stands, eyes blazing, two of her tremulous, tar-stained fingers pointing accusatorily at poor, pitiful Paul.

Gloria: Stands, though there is little difference from her sitting height. "Sit down, please!" Her voice is ludicrously high-pitched. Her look is determined, blindly righteous.

Shirley: "And you! You little rat! You're such a fake person! How can you live with yourself? Your squeaky little voice that never says anything! 'Squeak squeak squeak' just like a rat."

Dr. Comfort: "Please Shirley, please sit down. This is not good for you. You're much too excited." She looks over at Paul. "Did you give her her medication today?"

Paul: "Yes, this is what I've been telling you."

Shirley: "HE'S LYING! He never gave it to me, and you know it too!"

Dr. Comfort: "Please sit down, Shirley. Just for a moment, please."

Shirley: Sits down slowly and puts out her cigarette in the brass plated, circular ashtray on the table in front of her.

Dr. Comfort: "Now, you seem very angry, Shirley. What are you angry at? Are you angry at the people here, or are you angry at yourself? Which is it? Do you not like the people here or do you not like yourself?"

Shirley: "The people. They disgust me. And you, you disgust me, too, with your questions like you know something that I don't know. You're stupid. You don't know anything about me or about any of us. You come here once a month to sign release papers. That's all you do. That's all you can do, you senile old vulture."

Dr. Comfort: "Shirley, these opinions of yours are not good for you. These opinions of yours hurt people and they hurt you in return. Do you understand?"

Shirley: "Sure, sure I understand. I understand everything."

Dr. Comfort: "Good. So if you have these opinions, these bad opinions about people, you must, do you hear me, you must keep them to yourself or we're going to have to take you somewhere else to live. Can you keep your opinions to yourself? Can you do that for me? For all of us? Can you do that for yourself?"

Shirley: "And what about you?"

Dr. Comfort: "We're talking about you, Shirley."

Shirley: "No we're not, we're not talking about me at all, we're talking about you." She stands again, pointing accusatorily at them.

"And we're talking about you, and you, and you! You want me to shut up, then give me a pill. You want to send me back over there, then go ahead. Go ahead! That's what this is all about, isn't it? That's what it's all about with you people, isn't it? Sending us over there! You think we don't know! You think we're stupid. You play these games like you're trying to help us, but you don't care. You want to send us over there. Well go ahead! (Dr. Comfort begins scribbling on a clipboard.) That's right, sign the release if you can even sign your name you're so old and broken down. The only reason you got this job is because you're the only one who could be bought; it's the only job you're fit for . . . "

Paul and Gloria: Stand and walk around the table to her side. They try to gently lead her away from the table.

Shirley: "GET YOUR FUCKIN' HANDS OFF OF ME YOU SLIME! I know what you're doing, what you're all doing . . . "

Dr. Comfort: "Paul, get her medication."

The next day Shirley was gone. They had to handcuff her and posey her to a wheelchair, she put up such a fuss. Dorothy and I helped. When she was gone, Dorothy just shook her head sadly and said: "Shirley done it, Richud, she let the cat outa the bag. It gonna get mean from here on in. Jus' watch."

bobby

At fifty-two, Bobby was just two years old. His age, like his ugly puss, was a fixed part of him. He never developed a day beyond what he was, what he had always been taught to be. Bobby was found in a house alone with his ninety-five-year-old mother dead in her bed and stinking up the neighborhood. Later, when the police investigated the case, they found no record of Bobby's birth anywhere. The mother, a recluse for most of her adult life, had given birth to Bobby in the house unbeknownst to the world, and had kept him there, inside, his entire life. His father was unknown. Bobby had no teeth, and it was not known why. The Coroner's Office reported that the dead woman's body showed decades of breast feeding. Intelligence testing found no signs of physiological mental retardation. This deranged agoraphobic had conditioned her son to remain a two-year-old, and with no outside contact for fifty years, there was nothing to prevent it.

Bobby was a creature. He was tall, about six feet four, with long arms and legs that held no muscularity whatsoever. He had a pot belly even though his chest and back were slight of build. He had a huge nose, large ears, cross eyes, and about a twelve-inch-long tongue that delighted Paul to no end. He was quite spastic, and looked liked a praying mantis when he walked—his limp wrists allowing his hands to dangle in front of him as he shuffled along crying as he walked. He would cry without provocation exactly like a baby: "Wahnn Wahnnn . . . " This he did for attention or when he was tired or hungry. He could blow kisses, wave, hug and kiss, and say his name. In fact, he was echolalic. An echolalic is a person who repeats the last two syllables of whatever is said to him. That was Bobby.

Everyday he sat in a high-backed chair next to the nurse's station, and he'd bawl every once in a while just like John Brown would crow. It's funny, but I used to think of him and John Brown as the Alpha and the Omega respectively, for between them existed every manner of derangement—one the ultimate victim of circumstance, the other of teratogenetics.

On some days, Bobby would be a brat. He'd continually get out of his chair, walk over to someone eating or smoking, and smack him hard, then turn and scramble higgledy-piggeldy back to his seat, wailing as he went. Paul used to dote on Bobby and kept him close to his desk so that he was, in effect, invulnerable to reprisals. Bobby was fully aware of this fact and took advantage of it, attacking people only when Paul was in the room. Floyd, of course, was the exception. He hit Floyd once, right in the face, when Floyd was doing time posied to a nearby chair. Floyd didn't retaliate right away, but by the end of the day, after he had slipped his shackles, Bobby's nose was bloodied and his eye and lips were swollen. I never saw Bobby hit Floyd after that.

Bobby, true to his two-year-old comportment, was incontinent. He'd shit on himself with a vengeance. Maybe the reason I hated Paul so much was because he took such pleasure in alerting me to the fact that Bobby had had "an accident." I always wanted to grab Paul by the collar and scream into his fat effeminate face: "THERE'S NOTHING ACCIDENTAL ABOUT IT!" Of all the jobs, that was the worst. He'd cry and fight you and try to kiss and hug you while the crap was smeared all over his legs and butt and stinking to high Heaven.

It definitely affected my weltanschauung, having to change and diaper a fifty-two-year-old two-year-old. Nothing in my education, my readings, my religion classes prepared me for such a task. And sometimes I'd have to do it twice in one day.

Getting him up in the morning and dressed was the same as with any two-year-old. Somedays he'd be acquiescent and agreeable, other days he'd be a bear. On those days, Kelvin and I, together, with the door closed tightly, would manhandle him. That was actually fun, though we were always quite on edge that Paul would pop his head in the door to see how his baby was doing. We'd smack his ass good and threaten and cajole him and he'd cry and repeat—

"C'mon, get up." Smack! He'd slap a good one on his rump.

"Annh hahnn hahnn . . . et up." he'd sob.

"Be a man about yo'self and get outa that bed," Kelvin had no particular love for Bobby.

"At beh."

"C'mon bohy, get outa that bed o' I spank you good."

"You gooh."

"What's you name, bohy?"

"Bahbee."

"How ole you?"

"Do." He'd hold up two fingers, his eyes crossed, his head swaying from side to side.

"Give me a kiss."

"MMMWAH." Then Bobby would lean his ugly face and arms over the side rails of his bed to hug and kiss Kelvin who would take the opportunity to hoist him down so we could both work him over. He'd cry and protest like Baby Huey, but with the both of us working on him we'd get him changed and dressed in no time.

One day, however, during one of these strong-arm maneuvers, Bobby's nose got inadvertently broken. Getting Bobby to hug and kiss him as usual, Kelvin began to pull him off the bed when suddenly Bobby tried to get back into bed. The gravity and physics of it was all wrong and there was nothing we could do. He fell limply and smacked that huge nose against the tile floor with a crack. That event, just six months after my tenure began at the Rainbow, marked the beginning of the end for me. Kelvin got fired, and I got sent downstairs to the second floor to work with the adolescents. I was to be demoted one more time, but more on that later.

As I look back with heavy heart on what happened, I can't help but wonder why two years old? Why not four or five or ten? Why two? And harder still, how did she do it?

billy was a bad boy

So, down I descended. And as I went down through the building it became increasingly less humorous and more difficult to keep my chin up. Without Dorothy or Kelvin, I was truly on my own—I was like Dante without his Virgil alone in the Inferno.

Billy Bad Boy had epilepsy awfully bad. So bad in fact that he couldn't walk without a walker, he'd shit and piss on himself constantly, and all he did most of the time was laugh in a high-pitched shrill like a drunken leprechaun till you scolded him for it. But his epilepsy was a different kind—it was self-inflicted. See, he got into some bad trouble a few years back and when they put him behind bars he hanged himself. But, before he could swing into paradise, they found him. Dorothy told me the whole story, and how after they had pulled him down off the ceiling he had a seven-hour seizure. Seizures kill lots of brain cells, especially the seven-hour variety. Billy Bad Boy didn't have many brain cells left. In fact, he was, quite simply, a blithering idiot. But he wasn't always that way:

Billy Was a Bad Boy

Billy was a bad boy
Who didn't give a lick.
If his girlfriend made him angry,
He'd beat her with a stick.
He liked to rob the liquor stores
And steal fast cars and drink.
And he always made it tough for cops
To throw him in the clink.
He never worked, he only stole,
And slept most days till three.
He liked tatoos and hated Jews
And never once said "Pardon Me."
He was so short and scrawny,
And perhaps that was his beef,
Because he seemed determined
To cause the world much grief.
One night he came a callin'
On his girlfriend at her place.
He'd had a pint and felt all right
And had even washed his face.
The door was opened suddenly
By a lady twice his age.
It was his girlfriend's mother
Whose eyes were wide with rage.
She stood there in the doorway,
And cursed him up and down,
While he couldn't help from noticing
Her figure beneath her gown.
She really let him have it,
About all he'd said and done
To her one and only daughter—
She had three older sons.
Bad Billy wasn't listening,

He'd heard all this before,
So he looked around, then knocked her down
And closed and locked the door.
She put up quite a struggle
When he tried to lift her dress,
So he cracked her on the noggin'
The gash made quite a mess.
He dragged her to the kitchen,
And raped her on the floor.
And though she seemed half dead to him,
He raped her two times more.
He left her in the bathtub,
With a gag set tight in place.
He had a beer and then returned
To piss upon her face.
And as he gripped the doornob,
Much to his chagrin,
The door flew open suddenly
And his girlfriend walked right in.
She had a look of wonder
To see him in her flat,
Because she knew her mother
Wouldn't ask him in to chat.
She glanced about the living room,
And spied the telltale puddle.
Instantly she understood,
She wasn't the least befuddled.
She gave a mighty holler,
Hoping a neighbor would hear.
And as his fate would have it
A young officer was near.
He chased him through the alleys,
Round the town—right on his tail.
Finally he collared him

And dragged him off to jail.
There he sat in silence
Playing games inside his head;
Telling stories to himself,
And wishing he was dead.
He came upon a notion,
A capital one indeed.
The belt around his blue jeans
Was the only thing he'd need.
He strung it through the crossbars
Of that iron jailhouse door,
And he hung it high enough
So he couldn't reach the floor.
He got upon the bunkbed
And stretched himself across;
Put his head inside the strap
Then gave his legs a toss.
He dangled there forever,
And he barely made a peep.
Alas it just so happened—
Officer Monroe couldn't sleep.
On a whim he went to check,
And there he found him hanging.
He cut the belt with his knife,
And Billy Boy came down banging.
They rushed him by ambulance
To a hospital nearby.
But when they saw the damage,
They didn't bother to try.
Billy Bad Boy had a seizure
That continued through the night.
Seven hours long it lasted
Until the dawn's first morning light.
Well, the seizure killed his demons;

Never again will he be
Holding up a liquor store
Or threatening you or me.

So Billy Bad Boy was harmless. Strangely enough, his girl-friend, despite all that he had done to her, would visit him occasionally. She'd sit there holding his hand—he, laughing hideously—talking to him like a child:

"You really need a bath Billy. Oh, and momma says 'Hi.'"

the autistics
(get those kids some sneakers!)

I have a theory about autism. For some, the prospect of self-awareness is too profound, too terrifying, and the mind simply refuses to accept itself. What is thought, after all, but a constant interior mumbling of confusion, classification, judgment, and fear. So the idea "I am me" does not compute. In place of self-awareness, of "me" if you will, a pattern manifests itself. A good example of this replacement pattern theory of mine can be observed by watching the polar bear at the Central Park Zoo. That poor bear—one of the world's freest and most ferocious animals—trapped within the confines of a cell a few times his own size, has built a pattern around his incomprehensible realty. If you stand and watch him for a few minutes you would see him repeat the same exact body movements over and over again—side to side he rocks, then he scratches his back on the iron bars, dives into the water, comes up and swims on his back, drags himself out of the water, and returns to his original spot and starts over again. Hour after hour, day after day, year after year. Perhaps any daily routine, now that I think of it, is a form of this pattern replacement to avoid the terror of self-awareness.

We had two autistics—Rumeal and Birna. Rumeal was a black kid about seventeen, sinewy and short, who sat and rocked and jumped. Boy could that kid jump. Boing! Like a kangaroo. Birna was the same age, a white girl with sandy blond hair, and she rocked in time to the music on a little tape cassette she had—side to side, on one foot and then the other, her head swaying and her hair following an instant later. She was a safe autistic. Rumeal, on the other hand, would get out of control. He'd have these fits of leaping, and with all that furniture and the other kids around, it got difficult. Shit, he could jump right over a chair, backwards or forwards.

Devoid of facial expressions, unable to communicate, it became apparent to an unschooled worker like myself that the only means in which to interpret an autistic's feelings was by observing his pattern. As the weeks passed, and I became more and more familiar with Birna and Rumeal's patterns, I became aware of something. Their patterns seemed to hit a point during the day when they could no longer continue with any fluency. Every movement seemed forced and painful. Now an autistic is blessed with indefatigable energy, so the energy factor was out. What could it be that was upsetting both these patterned people so? Then the thought hit me—Get Those Kids Some Sneakers! Poor Rumeal wore those godawful loafers with thin leather soles; Birna wore simple canvas sneakers with very little support under the arches. Hell, those kids were putting incredible wear and tear on that footwear, and they needed the best.

I presented my idea to Gloria one day but she shooed me away with her polite, patronizing words, "Thank you for being so concerned, Richard. We all appreciate it. The children most of all, but it's just not in our budget at this time." What budget?

I was determined. Those kids had to get the proper footwear. Imagine Michael Jordan playing his game in a pair of shitty old loafers? And Rumeal was jumping every bit as much as Michael Jordan does on a daily basis.

A hundred and fifty bucks at least, I calculated. I obsessed on this idea. On my days off I would find myself at the nearest shoe store, pricing and comparing, thinking—"These are perfect for Rumeal." or "These have Birna's name written all over them." I had resolved to buy the shoes myself. Problem was, $150 was more than I had in my bank account. I had no money, but I had to buy those shoes if it was the last thing I would ever do!

I remember Kelvin had commented the day he was fired that he would get a job as a cabdriver, like his uncle. He said the money was good, and best of all you could get a job right away without need of recommendations and all that rigamarole. So I enrolled in the cabdriver's course. What a crock of shit that was. Eight hours on a beautiful Saturday sitting in a folding chair listening to a moron instruct you how not to drive a goddamn car—"Don't use the brakes unless you absolutely have to. Do you know how easily brakepads wear out?" "Pull down on your blinker signal, but not so far that it clicks, no use wearing out a perfectly good blinker. Just pull it down far enough for the light to work. Do you know how much it costs to repair a worn out blinker?" "Don't speed up and slow down, that's how the carburetors foul." Anyway, I endured it and I got the probationary taxi license. The gravy was that as a probationary cabby I was allowed three days to ply my trade without having to pay the fifty-dollar cab rental fee. It only took me two days to make the $150 bucks for the sneakers. That's the last time I'll ever drive a cab. Two days, ten hours at a pop, one entire weekend of sitting on my ass and trying to talk and understand cabbyspeak over a radio. What an argot that is. I must have picked up two dozen elderly alcoholics who just needed a lift around the corner to get another bottle of booze.

The day I brought the shoes in I simply told everyone that my next-door neighbor owned a shoe store and he gave me the shoes. Dorothy knew what was what. She winked at me when she heard my little spiel.

At the gift opening were Dorothy and Dorothy's sister Althea who worked on the floor with me some of the days. We brought those beautiful seventy-five-dollar-a-pair sneakers out of the boxes as if they were holy hosts. They certainly smelled like holy hosts, with the bright white laces all new and thick, the smell of rubber and foam and leather. . . . We put those sneakers on those kids like we were crowning a new king. Shoes in place, we stood back to watch our good deed unfold. The way they walked away at first was like watching a dog being let go after a bath. Both of them seemed so unsure, yet at the same time so lightfooted and free. Then the patterns started up—the bounces and the rocking and the jumping. What fluency they demonstrated. There were great big grins in those patterns.

"Tha's somethin' good right there, Richud. They know what you done, too. They know," Dorothy's sister Althea said.

Well, anyway, I didn't have to live with that preoccupation any longer.

waldo wong and things oriental

Waldo Wong was a seventeen-year-old Chinese-American who was coded as Emotionally Disturbed. He was epileptic, fastidious, creative, and last but not least, monomaniacal. His monomania, or his raison d'etre if you will was, incredible as it may seem, *Sports Illustrated* magazine. The magazine was at the very center of his being. The day before his admission into the Rainbow, Waldo was apprehended by police at 3:30 A.M., running down the frosty night street in his pajamas, his bare feet bleeding, and in his arms was the latest edition of *S.I.* His fixation had grown way out of control. He was spending most of his school time, during class and in between, poring over any *S.I.* he could get his hands on. His parents finally prohibited him from reading it, confiscated all of his back issues, and of course promptly cut off his subscription. Unable to stand it any longer, he jumped out of his bedroom window in the middle of the night and headed for the local library ten blocks away. Once there, he smashed in the window of the front door with a hammer he'd brought along for that very purpose, crawled in, and somehow found his beloved *S.I.* in the dark. So anxious to get back home to read it, he cut his feet on the broken glass in the process and was running down the street at a good clip when the police picked him up. That was one year before I came into his life. Of course by the time I came along any mention of the magazine around him was strictly forbidden.

A monomania is a beautiful thing to observe. Once you are aware of it you quickly realize that around the monomaniac his subject exists everywhere and in everything. Conversations are laced with it, and everyone then becomes a conspirator in his game. It's like a spell, when you're near him you're his for the taking.

The second floor was the adolescent floor. A motley bunch of autistics, epileptics, stutterers, Down's syndromes, idiots, and in my opinion—idiot savants. I was convinced that Waldo was one of the latter because of his ability to quote and recall passages and statistics from *S.I.* he'd read years before. He was a living, breathing encyclopedia of sports trivia. For example, if you wanted to know who were the top ten home run hitters of all-time he could spit that right out for you. If it had been printed in *S.I.* in the past five years, he could recite it verbatim. What a resource he was. Of course asking him questions like this was grounds for dismissal, according to the new case worker on the floor, Rose Wood.

Rose Wood was this overweight, unattractive, neurotic nurse about my age whom the administration hired to promote their cause. Yeah, Gloria and Big Bird were finally getting smart; at long last they realized the aides were important allies in their ploy. But the holdovers were not on their side, so Gloria and Big Bird began to fire them and bring in their own people. Kelvin's dismissal was an example of this new tactic as was Rose Wood's hiring. They only kept me because I looked good, i.e., the white male college graduate. But Rose Wood was the ultimate enemy. She was a know-it-all, she had eyes in the back of her head, and she ruled that second floor with a vengeance. The kids hated her, though she would be the last person to realize this fact. Like many people today, Rose Wood was in a job which unfortuately promoted her neurosis, i.e., her need to control all aspects of her life. It's impossible to control one's own life, then throw in thirty psychotic adolescents on top of that. I was certain that after a few years working there her family would be registering her in as a client. In any case, from the moment we met we were arch enemies.

Waldo Wong was my favorite. Every chance I got I talked sports with him. He absolutely glowed when I did this. He prodded me for news about the recently started baseball season because Rose Wood had forbidden him to read the sports section of the newspaper or watch sports on T.V. I used to take great pleasure in sneaking sports sections to him. He'd write these incredibly elaborate thank you letters with perfect penmanship and ornately drafted pictures of famous baseball players with their lifetime batting averages underneath. This he did under the cover of night because there is no way he could have done all that beautiful work with Rose Wood still on the prowl. His ecstacy absolutely ignited me.

Then he got caught. Rose Wood found the sports sections, and, amazingly, a couple of *Sports Illustrated* magazines hidden meticulously in a manila envelope behind one of the framed pictures on the wall of his room. She humiliated him in front of the others with unctuous and demoralizing words, and did her best to subjugate him like all things in her ken. He didn't betray me though, that heroic soul. He kept our secret, and although tortured beyond human endurance, he didn't crack but insisted that he stole the newspapers from the pipe-smoking paranoid on the first floor. Following this calumnation Waldo was depressed for weeks and I did my best to encourage him. At times he seemed to respond well to this encouragement, and after a little while an ember of his old ecstacy began to glow again. I felt proud of myself for bringing the old Waldo back.

Then one day his whole family came to visit him. What a breath of fresh air they were. They were a nice, bright, normal Chinese-American family with his brothers and sisters all honor students, and one brother an engineering major at M.I.T. I was instantly struck by how the parents and grandparents prattled on in Chinese. After they left I had to ask him:

"Wally, you speak Chinese, hunh?"

"Ahh Soo."

"Wow. Can you say a couple of things in Chinese for me? Like . . . um—"

"Rich, have you seen Terry?" Rose Wood broke in, looking for a client.

"Yeah, I think he's showering," I responded in the same breath, and away she went. "There, how about that one Wally," continuing. "Terry's showering? He's showering?"

"He showa."

"He showa . . . that's how you say it?" playing along with him. Of course he didn't speak of word of Chinese.

"Ahh Soo."

"That's great. Your grandparents don't speak a word of English I bet."

"Nah so."

"So were you born here or in China?"

"A Hong Kong."

"Hong Kong! I didn't know that. Well then, Ahh Soo to you too." And I bowed with my hands cupped before me in mockery of an oriental salute.

"Ahh Soo," he returned my bow and my greeting very deliberately and precisely, and I noticed immediately that his face began to beam the way it used to.

And so that was the very beginning of a whole new idée fixe. Waldo Wong became possessed by all things oriental—Chinese, Japanese, Korean, it didn't matter. I thought it was glorious and felt like a proud parent for having given birth to such a marvelous idea. Rose Wood was cognizant of his new tack almost the moment she laid eyes on him, and was in an absolute funk about it. At least before all she had to do was keep *S.I.* and the sports section out of his hands and everything was fine. But this . . . how, pray tell, could she keep a Chinaman from being Chinese?

Waldo was a masterpiece. He underwent the most exquisite metamorphosis. Gone were all the silly, suggestive pictures of sports on his walls, and in their stead were hung huge, pregnant pictures of Chinese dragons and Chinese writing and Chinese checkerboards. Two or three letters were being mailed daily to his grandparents, brothers and sisters, aunts and uncles to send all things oriental to him. And they did, for a while anyway. In no time at all he had a full wardrobe of things oriental, tapes of Chinese and Taiwanese pop music, posters and calendars and magazines and food and chop sticks. Even his hair he made look more Chinese. And all to the great chagrin of Rose Wood. In retrospect, I don't know if I admired Waldo's metamorphosis more for its grandeur, or because of what it did to Rose Wood.

Rose Wood fell under Wally's spell and began to realize there were things oriental everywhere. As I said, this was a very difficult problem for her because you can't, legally, keep a Chinaman from being Chinese. And Waldo knew this too. He knew he could flaunt his monomania with impunity, and he did so, much to my delight. Then she got down and dirty. First, she got rid of me. That was only a tiny fraction of it, but it was a start. She was smart enough to know that I had been aiding and abetting Waldo all along. They sent me down a floor again. Next, she brought the whole family in, sat them down, and delicately explained to them the situation. They listened and they understood. She won them over, that bitch. Yes, they knew Wally and they knew the degree of his monomanias.

The things oriental were removed immediately. His kimono was confiscated, as was all the rest of his collection. And behind one of the pictures on the wall they found the manila envelope stuffed full of labels from cans of La Choy Chop Suey, Chow Mein, Fried Rice, etc. along with magazine ads of same. It certainly looked like Rose Wood had conquered again, but I held onto one irrefutable conviction—they couldn't take the Chinaman out of him no matter how many things they took away from him.

It was a Sunday, and I was up on the top floor to retrieve a charge who had attended the Catholic mass up there. This was maybe five weeks A.C. (Anno Chinese). Waldo was up there reading something. I assumed implicitly that it was of an oriental bent. Rose Wood was nowhere in sight, so I caught his eye and bowed ever so discreetly to him. He returned my bow with a buck-toothed, magnanimous nod of his head. The television was blaring and I walked over to turn it down when I happened to notice Billy Graham pontificating about sin.

"You gettin' all of this, Wally?" I kidded him. Instead of laughing, he nodded humbly again. It was then that I noticed the quality of the nod to be different than before. It wasn't oriental at all, but a pious, omniscient nod. Suddenly, a moment later, leaning over his shoulder, I saw it! The Bible! Rose Wood was licked once and for all! Waldo was a genius!

cecelias 1, 2, and 3

So down into the final circle of Hell I descended. Of course who should I first meet upon entering that unholy realm, but the mother of all psychopathy—the multiple personality!

I had no idea what was going on down on the first floor, and no one made it a point to tell me, either. That's because no one down there cared. So long as the people paid their bills, that's all that really mattered. Gloria had her office on that floor so she was the de facto floor nurse in the morning. I was the only aide until twelve o'clock noon. After lunch there were two women who came on. I couldn't tell who was the aide and who was the LPN. In any case, it wasn't like the team effort we had on the third floor.

I had nothing to do on the first floor. All the clients were privates so they were voluntarily committed, which meant there was no coercion necessary. Coercion was 95 percent of the work on the third floor. My job on the first floor was more housekeeping than attending to personal care. I spent my time making beds, cleaning bathtubs, distributing lunches, and doing crossword puzzles.

Cecelia was about thirty years old, very plain looking. She had light blue eyes, very curly dirty-blonde hair that was always a mess, a smooth but pasty complexion. She was tall, five feet ten, and a good deal overweight—she probably weighed 180–190 pounds. Cecelia had three people inside her. I think three's a good number if you're going to be a multiple personality. With three you've got a built-in arbiter.

Cecelia paced the hall all day long with a cup of coffee, avoiding all eye contact and interaction with anyone. Round and round she'd go, growling lowly into her coffee mug. That was #1. Bluto I called her. During rows with #2, whom I named Popeye for obvious reasons, Cecelia would seclude herself in her room and go at it tooth and nail. As for #3 . . . she made only one very special guest appearance in my short time there. Before that encounter I had no idea there even was a #3. After I met her though, I convinced myself that #3 was the true Cecelia, the one who simply got overwhelmed and eventually tossed out of her own skull.

So there I was, my first day on the floor. I was in Cecelia's room making Cecelia's bed. At this point in time I took Cecelia at face value i.e., Bluto who paced the hall. But then #2 came along. Yes, Bluto and Popeye came disputing into the room. I had no idea what all the commotion was about. I thought at first she was cussing out one of the other clients for some reason or other. However, I can assure you that it doesn't take one long to descry a person angry from a person possessed. I slipped out of that room posthaste, my heart fluttering like a candle in the wind.

What can be said about a person arguing with herself in two different voices, other than that she needs to undergo an immediate exorcism. The Inquisition was right on that point.

In no time at all, this became quite routine. If I was in Cecelia's room making her bed and I heard the tell-tale caterwaul of Bluto and Popeye voicing their respective differences of opinions, I'd skeedaddle.

But then one day from out of the blue, just minding my own

business, sitting in the one vacant room I'd assumed as my own private headquarters, masturbating my mind over a Sunday crossword, Cecelia #3 walked into my life!

The door opened silently. I looked up and there she was, a sweet, demure expression on her face. She walked toward me, her hands clasped in front of her angelically. You can imagine the look on my face the closer she got because I was only used to anti-social Bluto marching the halls with that brutish countenance, surly as the day is long, or the ever-querulous Popeye. With soft as feather footfalls she floated ever closer to me, her hands clasped, the sweet, angelic expression unchanged. She stopped three feet from me and looked down at the Sunday magazine in my lap. Her sweet smile broadened—

"I've been wondering what you do in here, Richard. Crossword puzzles." Then with bent head, she turned and floated out the door, never to reappear again.

How is it that we've been blessed with such aberrations? It's almost too much for a human being to bear. Science is trying desperately to answer this question via microscopic examinations of our precious bodily ingredients. Will the day ever come when, with grease-stained hands, one of these big-headed boffins holds up to the light, squeezed between the tines of his pinchers, the little DNA culprit of mulitple personalities? If perchance he does, I personally would like to propose that a decree be issued on the spot to the effect that a world-wide holiday be observed to commemorate that day.

bette davis eyes

Shelly Mandel was an embarrassment. You would never think that to look at him. What a dresser he was. The whitest shirts you ever saw, silk ties, angora wool sweaters, Italian leather shoes. He was a true aristocrat. So what was a rich old Jew doing in a place like this? They were hiding him. Of course the administration was certain he was there because of the new wallpaper and the fish tank and the Rainbow. No, the fools didn't realize that Shelly Mandel was there because no one of his ilk would ever come across him in a place like this in this part of town—he was being stowed in an out-of-the-way place.

It made you sick to see Gloria and the rest of them cater to him like he was a king, which is exactly how he regarded himself. They had his shirts sent out to the dry cleaner twice a week. They let him smoke his cigars in his room and degrade the aides. And absolutely everything in that place, I soon realized, was done with Shelly Mandel or Shelly Mandel's family, rather, in mind. Behind every thought, every action at the Rainbow was the one question—"What would Shelly's people think if they saw this?"

Well, Shelly's people couldn't have cared less. They just wanted him out of their lives and in some out-of-the-way place. He did have one loyal sister. She would come every couple of weeks to take him to lunch or out shopping for a new tie. It was quite a sight to see that old fossil pull up in her Mercedes right out front. The chauffeur would open all the doors for her. Boy did she have the make-up caked on her puss. And you could smell her a mile away and for hours afterwards, she wore so much perfume. And jewelry! Expensive-looking stuff. Hell, she was a walking museum piece—both anthropologically and artifactually.

So she would come and the two old coots would shuffle out of the place, Shelly with his silk hanky fluffed up high, the sister's driver holding open the front door for them. Then away they'd drive. I remember when I was up on the third floor with Kelvin and Dorothy—we used to watch them from the window. Dorothy'd chuckle:

"Looky her hair now. Tha's a wig. Las' time it was blon' hair, now it brunette. Prob'ly gots herself a nigger to put it on in the mo'nin'."

"How much money you think she have in her purse ri' now?" Kelvin would wonder out loud.

"She don' have money in her purse chile, she keeps it all in the bank. Woman like dat use the plastic card."

"She a fool!" Kelvin would suddenly push himself away from the window, pissed that such an idiotic person could possess so much more than he.

But Shelly was an embarrassment. At 7:15 he came out of his room all shaved and dressed. He would immediately walk out of the building and onto the front steps where he'd find his paper, the *Wall Street Journal*. Back inside, he would return to his room, light up a cigar and wait for breakfast. I would serve his breakfast around 7:30 and he would always look at his gold pocket watch and shake his head no matter what time I brought it. He called me boy, which was okay because I looked more like thirteen than twenty-three.

"Put it over there, boy," he would point to his T.V. tray even though I put it there every day. He would go over all of the food as if it were diamonds he had ordered and was making sure everything was there. And even though everything was there, it was never good enough. He'd pick up the empty glass on the night stand next to him and shake it saying, "Water!" So I'd fill his glass with water and wait. He'd point to his dirty white shirts and I'd pick them up and shlepp them down to the office.

Shelly had no redeeming qualities because he was a solipsist and treated no one like a human being. We were all servants and he was the one and only. Had Queen Elizabeth herself walked into his room, he no doubt would have requested that she shine his shoes. Shelly's imperiousness, his total lack of regard for other human beings was the reason for his institutionalization. To me this was the ultimate abuse of the system. For someone who had plenty of money, who could afford to be administered to at home privately, to be placed in a facility simply because he was an embarrassment was a slap in the face to the mission of mental health.

Shelly and the black folks didn't get along. In fact, in retrospect, I believe I was kept on at the Rainbow specifically because of Shelly—the entire time I was there I was slowly being groomed to be his slave. The administration knew that no self-respecting black person would go near that man. His name was taboo amongst them. Psychotic or not, no black person in his right mind would step back a century to play slave to a white, bullying master—not that I loved playing the part any more than they, mind you.

After breakfast Shelly drew his pictures. Every picture was the same person, just the hairstyle or the clothing was different. Everyone had Bette Davis eyes. And one day it hit me, he had Bette Davis eyes himself. Nothing against Bette Davis, but I quickly came to hate Bette Davis eyes. To me they represented total egocentricity, solipsism. Shelly Mandel was a true solipsist—the one and only. Of course that's redundant, a solipsist is always the one and only. I'd always thought that solipsism was a neat idea, an interesting concept, but that was until I had met Shelly.

After lunch Shelly would sit out in the hall and play solitaire. That's a solipsist's favorite game. I asked him once if he wanted to play gin or something. He didn't even acknowledge me.

I hated that old Jew. I think it's a natural reaction to hate anyone who has an air of superiority. Every day I wanted to bother that bastard. So one day I just started talking to him:

"Nice sweater, Shelly. Where did you get it?"

No answer.

"Nice tie, Shelly. How much did you pay for it?"

No answer.

"The four of clubs is open, Shelly. You got the three of diamonds free down there."

I pestered him as best I could almost every day but without a response. Then it happened, I got a reaction. I made some idle comment, I don't even remember what it was, and he suddenly bolted to his feet, his Bette Davis eyes cold and glassy:

"Do you insist on this game!" He bellowed. I froze. I had never heard him raise his voice before. The tone and quality of his words were so thoroughly dictatorial, authoritarian. "I have been insulted by far better than you!" he continued. "If you don't have the money then I suggest you get a lawyer!" It got weirder. "Five hundred thousand is the going rate for a load of tropical hardwood. If I don't have the money in three days, I'll own you. Now good day, sir."

Perhaps Shelly never got that $500,000 for the load of tropical hardwood. Maybe he ended up owning that man. Who knows. Personally, I think Shelly Mandel was always the same, solipsistic, egocentric person. How else does a person amass millions? I think that finally one day people got together and said, "Shelly, fuck you!" And like the emperor's new clothes, it was all over. He was an embarrassment!

I never bothered him again.

charmegne

I couldn't help but feel that I was betraying the cause, and Kelvin and Dorothy and all who'd been expunged by remaining there on the first floor. It was obvious that they kept me on because of Shelly, and because of the image I portrayed to the prospective clients' families. In fact, in my mind, I had become for them the very symbol of the chimeric reformation they envisioned for the facility—a young, white, college graduate, male nurse's aide. The first floor had become almost exclusively private clients by the time I arrived. It smelled nicer, it looked better with its obtrusive potted plants, wallpaper, and the garish tank of tropical fish above the nurses' station. This sham was complete in every way except for one minor fact, it was still a bughouse.

Things were certainly going their way. Gloria was almost always smiling whenever I'd see her. And she had good reason to—they had completely decimated the old guard up on the third floor, and as the weeks went on it seemed more and more prospectives came traipsing through the halls, eyeing me and all the other absurdities. One day as she led a very pleasant but care-worn-looking middle-aged woman through the hall, I couldn't believe it, Gloria came right up to me with an attitude of effusive comradery:

"And this is our Richard," putting her sweaty little paw on my shoulder, "the regular aide on the floor. Your son will even have someone his own age to talk to." The thought gave me the creeps—a male client my own age in that place, what a sentence.

The floor was more spacious, I will say that, because all of the rooms were singles. Whereas there were about thirty clients on each of the above floors, there were no more than a dozen on the first floor which, when you think about it, plainly illustrates the profit margin between a private and a Title XIX client. Strange as it may sound, the privates were actually the misfits. There was Cecelia of course, several elderly blind people, Merry Mary, a schizophrenic man who stared out the window all day smoking a pipe, several miscellaneous eccentrics, two Alzheimer's clients, and the meticulously dressed Shelly Mandel. And then there was Charmegne.

Charmegne was about twenty-five with long, silken, jet black hair. She was very vampish, but amply proportioned with fat cheeks, round little buttocks, a ski jump nose, and long bony hands with inch-long fingernails. She wore thick, purple rimmed glasses and gobs of make-up—very bright pastel colors like mauve and rose and fuscia. She was a schizophrenic, a nymphomaniac, a chain smoker, a liar, a thief, and a "nigger hater." She was trouble from the word go. She used to come up to the third floor occasionally when I was working there to solicit me, but Dorothy or Kelvin would toss her ass out of there as soon as they saw her. She used to scream at them and call them "dirty, stinkin' niggers." It was awful. Kelvin really used to get upset, but Dorothy would hush him up with reason: "Don' be listenin' to her. She ain' right in her mine, chile. She don' know what she doin'."

Charmegne might not have known what she was doing, but she certainly did as she pleased. She took advantage of her schizophrenia, and zealously adhered to the notion that the great thing about being crazy was that you could do and say whatever you wanted. This was especially true for a private, ambulatory client at the Rainbow. As such, she could come and go at will, there were no rules or regulations for her ilk. She got up late in the morning, ate some junk food, then hopped on a bus and turned tricks for free downtown at the mall. They put her on the pill and were constantly taking blood samples to make sure she wasn't infected with some nasty disease. But after I showed up on the floor, she stopped going downtown and started chasing me around.

She'd stand in her doorway with a cigarette in her hand staring smugly at me. It's a hard thing to assimilate, having a fairly attractive woman, albeit psychotic, who wants nothing else from you but to suck your cock, yet you know that from whatever angle you look at it, it just won't work. You play it over and over in your mind, but there is no consciencing intercourse of any kind with a person like that. And on top of that, I had to put up with a lot of abuse. At first it was typical stuff you hear on the streetcorner: "You sure look lonely today," or "Come into my room for a minute, I've got something to show you," or "You're a cutey, you know that?"

Then she started getting more aggressive and lascivious. She was leaving off wearing a bra, and I'd come walking innocently around a corner with a towel over my shoulder and shaving gear in my hand and there she'd be, waiting for me with her breasts as welcoming mats: "You can fuck me anytime you want," or "I'll bet it's big and fat, just the way I like it," or "I like to swallow, you know."

I complained to the office, but they had bigger problems than mine. Gloria, the idiot, suggested I tell her I was engaged.

Then it got downright dirty. Mr. Bette Davis Eyes had just finished his bath and I was on my hands and knees scrubbing down the tub, which was my usual line of work after a client took a bath, when I heard the door close and lock with a click. I looked up and Charmegne was standing there in a white, fluffy soft bathrobe which she quickly let slip to the floor. She stood there naked, smirking down at me.

I stood up immediately and tried to make light of it. "Well, I guess you're going to take your bath now," I remember saying as I smacked my hands together playing the undistracted worker part to the hilt. She said nothing and moved around the tub to me. Her eyes were intense, her nipples erect and hard as teeth. Spurning a naked woman is no mere trifle, let me tell you, schizophrenia or no schizophrenia. She reached up to grab me.

"Excuse me," I said and dodged her arms and skipped around to the other side of the tub. The tub was definitely an ally.

"Why won't you fuck me?" She was angry. She came around the other side of the tub and grabbed me desperately and stuck her tits up under my chin.

"Charmegne, let go," I instructed, now playing the role of an official. She stood steadfast. "Let go, please," this time more authoritatively. Nothing doing. She stood there wanting it, and nothing was going to dissuade her from her just dessert. Then I had a thought. I began to kiss her. This was working. She greeted my lips passionately, with her tongue fighting against my tongue in a battle of supremacy for the inside my mouth. God her breath stunk from all that tobacco. But the trap was set. I began to unzip my pants. Then I stopped suddenly—"Do you have a bag?"

"Hunh?"

"A rubber? I don't have a rubber. I always use a rubber," I said sincerely.

"Don't you have one in your wallet?"

"No, I'll get one, I know where I can get one." I felt her eyes burning through me. Then I felt the hands let go. "I'll be right back."

"Hurry," she sighed.

That night I decided to hand in my two-week notice at the end of the week. At twenty-three and a college diploma in my back pocket, I was free to move on to greener pastures at any time, Nick the Barber or no Nick the Barber. Providence, however, had something to say about that line of thinking.

The next day a new client arrived. Teddy Gail, a twenty-four-year-old traumatic brain-injured private, took up residence across the hall from Charmegne. We were a match made in Heaven, he and I, but more on that later. Anyway, he was like a built-in defence mechanism against Slutsy across the hall. She couldn't pull any of her tricks with Teddy and me hitting it off just a step away and receiving all that obsequious attention that the adminstration was wont to afford any new private.

One thing I never gave Charmegene enough credit for was the fact she was lazy. She didn't like waiting or working too hard for anything. She slept as long as she felt like, ate only what she desired, and had sex as frequently as possible. Basically she was a hedonist. She liked the idea that she could get what she wanted without having to travel all the way downtown for it. That was why she chased me so doggedly. And that's why it made perfect sense that within a fortnight she was found on top of Teddy, screwing his lights out, crippled though he was.

life in the rainbow

Up until I had been demoted to the lower two floors, I had managed to remain emotionally aloof. It was easy up on the third floor because it was like Dorothy said—"Richud, don' be tryin' to figure these folks out now, you gets yo'self a headache 'cause they all jus' crazy." That was an undeniable truism which went a long way in distancing the caregivers from their charges. But things changed when I worked with the kids. In Waldo Wong I found an ecstacy akin to my own, one-track minded though it was. And when I realized they wanted to end his great passion for their own peace of mind, I was no longer aloof. One thing about Waldo Wong, however, he still remained within the purlieus of Dorothy's epigram. But not Teddy.

Teddy Gail, at twenty-four, was every bit my peer. He was white, a high school graduate, and a mechanic by trade. He had had a traumatic brain injury a little less than a year before from a motorcycle accident. His brain had been scrambled badly, yet inside the man, underneath all the disability, the ataxia, apraxia, and aphasia, Teddy Gail, or a new version of Teddy Gail, was gestating. When we met there was a tacit understanding of everything almost immediately.

Teddy was in a wheelchair, his right side paralyzed and

curled like the nutant sag of an unfurled flower. His left side was functional, but awkward, lacking all fine motor movement. He wore a black eye patch over his right eye because he had double vision.

He couldn't talk, or rather he couldn't articulate his thoughts. He moaned and made deep guttural noises like cave men must have done before the invention of language. In sum, Teddy Gail was trapped inside a body and mind that didn't work the way it was supposed to, and he was cognizant of the fact.

In order to deal with this reality, Teddy acted like a twelve-year-old boy most of the time. He laughed uproariously at the most trifling things, he masturbated constantly, and he teased people mercilessly. As I said, this was all an act of sorts to help him keep his sanity. The doctors, however, believed the behavior had to do with the accident. As they put it in the chart: "His behavior is the manifestation of memory consolidation and shrinking, retrograde amnesia bla bla bla . . ." I had a tough time swallowing any of that hocus pocus because first of all, I implicitly understood Teddy's true state of mind, and second, even science is a moron when it comes to the workings of the brain. I believe that, like God, the brain will remain unknowable until the end of time. That's my hope anyway.

So Teddy and I became friends—or playmates is a better way of putting it. We had a gay old time, wheeling around the halls making believe we had something to do. We harassed Charmegne and Merry Mary, Cecelias #1 and #2, and Gloria. We blew spitballs through straws at anyone who walked into our scope, we blew up condoms and let them bounce around the halls, we set wastebaskets on fire, put lubricated condoms on doorknobs, turned the clocks back an hour, stole files and hid them. Whatever mischief we could think of, we did. I never got in trouble because this was all perfectly acceptable behavior—Teddy was a private.

There were times of deep depression for Teddy, however.

They came on fast and furiously and chilled me to the bone. We'd be laughing and making merry one minute and then all of the sudden that lone eye would flash, cloud over and storm. He'd insist on returning to his room. There he'd crawl into his bed like a wounded dog, and yowl at me to close the door. Hours would pass and still he'd be in the same exact position, the one eye staring blankly up at the ceiling, his good hand held with the backside against his forehead.

The halcyon days we spent together, menacing the halls, began to jade. There's just so much you can do on a single floor of a psychotic-infested building. A young man of twenty-four is meant to be out in the jungle, matching his wits and strength against the elements and beasts. I guess, in a way, he was his own beast and his own jungle, though his wits and strength were severely defective. He was such a noble soul, a heroic soul, greater than any I had ever known or read about. The battle raging inside him was cataclysmic, yet he managed to keep most of it hidden from view. Even his envy of me was extremely difficult to discern—noticeable only in the blink of an eye when I might bend down to tie my shoe or look at a clock near the end of the day. On his walls the social worker had hung up empowering, optimistic adages and pictures— "The sky's the limit," "Anything is possible," "Be all you can be," ad nauseum. But he believed in those quotes.

As the result of recent advancements in emergency medical treatment applied at the scene of an accident and in trauma centers, people who would have died ten years before were living. Thousands upon thousands of these brain-injured people were out there living in places where they didn't belong. And he had no reason being in a place like that, but then again where does one with such a condition belong? Who knows how many of them were atrophying in hospitals, nursing homes, or walking the streets in search of food or their old identities. Later on I was to find out the exact answers to these questions. But in just the short time that I had spent working with Teddy, I began to understand the mind-set of that pro-found injury, i.e., the victim must constantly try to accept the fact that the old self is dead. That is what Teddy's depressions were about, that is what made him act the way he did. He was grieving for an old friend whom he'd lost and couldn't seem to find—himself.

Gloria found Teddy fucking Charmegne, or Charmegne was fucking Teddy I should say, during one of Gloria's surprise, midnight inspections. For some reason, this was a big deal. I remember walking into the room the morning after the event. Teddy looked penitent; his mother was there, Teddy's neuro-psychologist was there, Charmegne's shrink was there, Gloria was there along with Big Bird herself, filling up the room. Teddy raised his arm for a high five, which I gave him, not realizing how inappropriate it was at the time. They were conferring about the whole ordeal, concerned about "Teddy's safety, his rehabilitation, his sanity." On that point they were right. I spoke up, too. I told them just what I thought about their putting him in a place like that. I didn't care that Big Bird was there, I was only thinking of Teddy. I offered them a true layman's perspective. And they listened to me, lowly nurse's aide that I was, or at least Mrs. Gail did.

That afternoon Mrs. Gail came out of a meeting with the doctors and the administrators and came right over to me. "I'd like to thank you for being so honest in there. I agreed with everything you said. I don't listen to those people anymore. In fact I've decided to take him out of here. I just didn't want to put him in one of those head injury factories. I thought it would somehow be nicer for him here. But he should be living at home now, I don't care what they say. No more institutions. I would like to ask you if you would consider being Teddy's personal care attendant at our house. I can pay you twelve hundred dollars per month, room and board included. I'll have to check with the insurance company, but I think we could also get you health benefits and a car." What was there to think about?

One week later I was wheeling Teddy out the front door in exaltation. Behind us, in the doorway of the office, stood the angry-eyed Big Bird, her huge avarian frame suddenly so absurd and innocuous. And frozen in disbelief at the behemoth's side, stood the rodent-toothed Gloria. It was the one great victory, our Little Big Horn, if you will. We didn't win the war, but we won that battle. If only Kelvin and Dorothy and all of them could have been there to watch the faces of Gloria and Big Bird. I wanted so badly to flip them the bird, but my sense of propriety held me back.

"I implore you, Mrs. Gail, Dr. Comfort as well as Teddy's own doctor both feel quite strongly that you will be compromising his development by putting him in the hands of a non-professional," Big Bird reasoned as we headed out her office door.

"I couldn't agree more," said Mrs. G., turning with a theatric grace. "That's why I'm taking him out of here and home where he belongs. We're all professionals there, even Richard." That snapped the towering ostrich's head back.

Charmegne came out to see us off, as did Merry Mary. They had been waiting at the door the entire time we were in the office. Merry Mary thought I was going on vacation with Teddy—that's what I had told her. Outside the sun was shining, the birds were chirping, Lake Michigan was scintillating in between the wall of buildings in front of us. It was a glorious day, a victorious day. I rolled him down the ramp and away from the building, out from under that multicolored arc.

"Bye Richard dear. I'll miss you so much. Write me a postcard, please," Merry Mary said, clinging tightly to my arm with tears in her eyes. I pried her loose and pushed her back toward the steps.

Charmegne just stood there on the patio nodding, holding her cigarette up to her mouth, her lips parted to accept it. Then she pulled it away suddenly, "Hey Teddy, you're a good fuck," she said, and turned and walked back to her life in the Rainbow.

bella napule
(nine months later)

"Ha ha, 'at's'a my buddy, get up'a dere, Nick take'a care you. Been long time."

"I've been really busy."

"I bet. How's'a you buddy doin'? Nice boy," tossing an apron over my torso.

"Doin' well, doin' well, Nick. He got the eyepatch off, you know—the diplopia's gone. Hey, you won't believe this, but he's actually going to enroll in college. Wants to be a journalist."

"College? 'At's'a somet'in', hunh? *Madonna*," honing, unconsciously, the razor on the strap attached to the barber's chair.

"It's this newsletter we've put together, it's got him all pumped up. He's really changed. He's just really into what we're doing. It's been the perfect thing for him."

"What's'a dis now?"

"I didn't tell you about the Survivor's Ink newsletter?"

"No! You no tell'a me nothing. I no see you in'a long time, buddy. I don' even see you since Christmastime, it's'a ready May now."

"I guess you're right. Well, we started a newsletter, like a little newspaper, that goes out to all the survivors of TBI. We've built up quite a network of names—"

"TBA, what's'a dat?"

"TBI—traumatic brain injury. That's what they call it. And remember, the 'survivors' always goes before the TBI—you say, 'survivors of TBI'; not vice versa, makes it clear to everyone that these are first and foremost people and not injuries. But this newsletter thing . . . we publish articles written by survivors who tell us their stories, mostly about how they've been treated or ripped off. You wouldn't believe some of the stuff we get, the stories. He writes a column, Teddy does. I do all the editing and layout. It's going out over the Internet; we've got our own E-mail address and everything. You should see the computer and the printer the Gails bought us."

He walked over to the sink and got a comb, came back and started running it through my long tangled mass. "Hair long, healthy. So you gotta newspaper you write wit'a you buddy? Maybe you start some'ting for'a youself now. Dis sounds'a good, maybe become big'a newspaper man; you get rich an'a famous."

"Hardly. The only people gettin' rich and famous are the hospitals and homes who treat these people. You wouldn't believe the stuff going on, Nick. You wouldn't believe it. You talk about cold-hearted rip-off. Man, The Rainbow was nothing compared to this. And money . . . You just wouldn't believe the money they're raking in. Billions of dollars! They're makin' billions of dollars on this TBI thing now. It's the scandal of the century! Get this: they went from six TBI facilities nationwide about six years ago, to over four hundred today. It's the rip-off of the century, I'm telling you! Because ten years ago people like Teddy died. Now with all this new technology, all this emergency medical treatment, the 911 system, people are surviving by the thousands, by the tens of thousands! New facilities are opening daily. They're calling it, TBI, the silent epidemic. A million survivors a year, Nick, and all twisted and mangled and demented and in need of care. Sound familiar? Forget about the private mental facility business, that's peanuts compared to this stuff. Do you know how much these facilities are making? Take a guess?"

"Can't'a guess, got no idea."

"Acute TBI care runs at least $2,500 a day and in some cases as much as $10,000! It's unbelievable! Post-acute care is like $1,000 a day. Exploitation, goddamn it. I'm sick of it. Why is there so much exploitation, Nick? Why is it when someone really needs help, is completely dependent upon someone else, there's always someone else on the scene making a sinful amount of money off of it?"

"It jus'a way it is. Like'a Darwood, survival of the fastest."

"Yeah. Anyway, I'm leaving in two weeks. As soon as school starts for him, I'm done. The Gails know all about it. In fact they've encouraged me, given me a bonus." I stopped and waited for him to say something, but he continued to cut my hair. "Know what I'm gonna do, Nick? I'm g—"

"—goin' finish'a dee walk," he completed the sentence with a knowing gleam, popping his head up from the back of my neck where he had been snipping furiously.

"Yeah. How did you know?"

"But you not'a goin' go Alaska dis'a time, right?"

"That's right." I thought I was going to surprise him and he turned around and beat me to the punch.

"So where'a you goin' go, my buddy?" He stopped cutting and looked at me in the mirror with great expectation.

I took a deep breath. "It goes something like this, Nick: 'I believe there is a subtle magnetism in nature which will direct us aright. It is not indifferent to which way we walk, there is a right way, but we are very liable from heedlessness and stupidity to walk the wrong way.' Thoreau again."

"So which'a way you goin' go?"

"Your way, Nick. I'm going to Italy. I've arranged to hop a freighter in New York and work my way to Naples, your hometown."

"*Napule! Porco dio! Non te muor'e friddo li.*"[1] He stood there beaming proudly at me in the mirror as if I were his newborn child and he were looking at me through the big glass window. "*Bella Napule! Bella Napule! Che bravo!*" he said, shaking his head wistfully.

"I write'a my brother. He's garbage collector, work'a for dee city. He no speak'a English, but he know lot's people. Get'a you job, have you a'working, right 'way."

"In Naples?"

"*Si, bella Napule.*"

---

[1]You won't die from the cold there.

A NOTE ON THE AUTHOR

RICHARD HORAN has worked as a professional boxer, a nurse's aide, a high school baseball and football coach, and a teacher. He currently teaches English in Seoul, Korea. His wife Mary is a jazz vocalist and they have two daughters. *Life in the Rainbow* is Horan's first book.

A NOTE ON THE BOOK

This book was composed by Steerforth Press using a digital version of Galliard, a typeface designed by Matthew Carter based on the designs of sixteenth-century Parisian typecutter Robert Granjon, and issued by Mergenthaler and ITC in 1978. The book was printed on acid free papers and bound by Quebecor Printing ~ Book Press Inc. of North Brattleboro, Vermont.